MW01490868

MANY A TEAR HAS TO FALL

*One Man's Struggle
Through the
Death of a Dream*

Wayne Hudson

*Padon Press
Vancleave, MS*

For my wonderful daughter....
The love of my life,
Casey

Acknowledgements

My sincere thanks to everyone who took an interest in this project supporting me with encouraging words and in some cases, hard work.

A very special thank you to Dr. Yeager Hudson, B.A. Millsaps College, S.T.B. and Ph.D. Boston University, Charles A. Dana Professor Emeritus, Colby College, retired United Methodist Minister, author and editor of numerous books and articles. I will forever be indebted for the countless hours spent editing, proofreading, correcting, challenging me.

Also to Nelda Davis, who out of her love for the Lord and compassion for an author in great need of her talents, gave her time and encouragement to this project.

I am grateful to David Pierce who at just the right time, offered just the right support and advice. It was inspiring to watch someone so willing to be used by God to help and encourage one who needed it so desperately.

Finally, a heartfelt thanks to those willing to tell their stories in the chapter entitled, *"Conversations with the Wounded."* Your contribution was far above all expectations.

Contents

Introduction

We hear from so many sources that the family is an endangered institution. We believe that God ordained it, created it, and for thousands of years, has blessed it. Yet it seems as if man has been bent on devising more and more ways of destroying the family. It is like a paradox. Even from childhood, nearly everyone dreams of being a part of this basic unit of our society. However, most put very little effort into preparing themselves for marriage, and once they have a family of their own, many seem ready to allow the most trivial reasons to break up their family. It is as if we think marriages and families are disposable—like so many used paper plates. It is my hope that this book can help people who have not given much thought to the importance of family life. It is also written for those who might not realize there are tried and proven ways to strengthen the family and to find the joy it was intended to have. For persons who may be struggling to save their family from becoming just another statistic, I would like this book to offer hope and a measure of guidance in that struggle.

Marriages, even troubled ones, can be saved, and I am convinced that they are worth putting forth a very great effort. This book is also addressed to those persons who have already experienced the tragedy of a divorce and are trying to come to terms with the aftermath. You will see various stages one passes through and may even recognize where you are in this process. Once you do, you can read on to learn what is next and how to cope. One of the most difficult issues may be that of child custody—especially for the individual who has to learn to be a non-custodial parent.

Many A Tear Has To Fall ..... tells the story of someone

who has dealt with most of the very difficult aspects of divorce. There are important lessons to be learned from each one. Sharing these lessons can be a source of great comfort and can cause us to shift our focus from ourselves to others. Life is a wonderful journey and even in the worst of times, we can discover opportunities to help and minister to one another.

Though scripture makes it clear that God hates divorce, it is just as clear that He still loves the divorced persons. For those who cause the breakup of a family, He offers forgiveness. For the ones who have tried so very hard in vain to save their marriage, God offers hope for a meaningful life even after divorce. For the precious children of divorce, I believe that God Himself probably sheds *"many a tear."*

You may be asking yourself why anyone would have the audacity to think that his story, one that resembles that of thousands of others, would be worthy of presenting in a book. And more importantly, why would anyone want to bare his soul to so many? My response is that I feel God can use my tragedy to help others find their way through the harsh and lonely journey of divorce and to the place of healing and wholeness. I seem to always be meeting people for whom the trauma of divorce is excruciating. These are people whom God truly loves. I am so convinced that He has called me to this task that I have spent well over a year of my life writing this—my story.

Many a Tear Has to Fall is a story about people, very ordinary people. It is also a message of hope. More importantly, it is a story about an awesome God; one who is patient, loving and good! As you read this book, please remain open to what God might say to you about your own situation. If you really listen intently, He may reveal to you unspeakable and magnificent things about your life and your future. There are only two paths to take. First, you may choose the way that God has designed for you to go. Along this path you can ultimately expect to find the happiness and meaning that your life was meant to have. Like many others before you, it could be that you are tired of trying to make it purely on your own; tired of the uncertainty of not knowing which way to turn; and tired of feeling alone and that no one cares.

Perhaps the day will come sometime in the future when you will look back on this moment. When that time comes, what will you see? Will it be a time when you decided to make God a central part of your life so that he might lead you onto the right path? Or will it be a time when you see that you took the other path; a path filled with missed opportunities and regrets. When we choose this second path, we allow our lives to drift with no real sense of direction. It is my prayer that you will choose the first path, the path designed by God, and that this book will make some small contribution to your decision.

For the person whose life has been turned upside down and torn to shreds by a shattered relationship, truly, *Many A Tear Has To Fall*; but God is always there to dry every tear and offer a new beginning to all.

I

Reality Bites
Coming to Terms with the State of Affairs

It seems as though it's extra dark tonight. Usually the moon shines through the window softening the darkness. As I feel my pupils expanding, I think that this must be what it feels like to be blind. All of the sudden the headlights of a car break into the darkness, and I can see again. My heart starts pounding and thoughts begin to flood my mind. Could it be her? Is she finally coming home? If so, how should I respond this time? Should I meet her at the door with a righteous anger, or should I stay in bed pretending to be asleep and avoid a confrontation? Oh well, it doesn't matter; the car kept going. What time is it anyway? I look at the clock and it reads 1:45 AM. This is the most miserable I have ever been in my marriage.

In the next room is the apple of my eye. Casey is the most beautiful, happiest, and most energetic little 8-year-old girl ever. She is my joy and my life. She seemed oblivious to any problems her mother and I were having. I was happy about that, at least. At the time of her birth, I felt sure that our lives would settle down, and we would not have the problems that had riddled our marriage for years. I thought that this little girl would be the common denominator that would make our family important enough to work through anything that came our way.

When my daughter was born, due to medical complications, I brought her home a few days before my wife was released. As nervous and anxious as I was about this, I was equally excited and happy. This would possibly prove to be one of the most important times in our relationship as a father and daughter. It was during this brief time when I was totally responsible for her care and welfare that I bonded in a unique way with her. From that point on, she was my focus. I reordered my life around her and knew in my heart that this was a very special little girl. I marveled at her every move and the sounds she made. I was such a proud father and always eager to show her off. As she grew older, we remained inseparable, and with the exception of the time I spent at my job, it seemed that we were always doing something together. She was about three when something happened that radically changed my life and my perspective.

A New Creation

I was working late one night with a friend. The others had gone home and the two of us finally sat back to relax for a moment before leaving. My friend had been attending a revival at his church that week and was on a spiritual high. We began talking about religion, church and the Bible. He inquired about my spiritual life and finally asked if I was a Christian. I remember thinking what a surprising coincidence since I had been giving this subject a lot of thought lately. I had known from the time when I was young that I needed to be saved from myself and my sin. Yet as an adventurous man in my early twenties, Christianity was just about the last thing on my mind. Once married, I quickly changed and settled down. I had always wanted a nice, wholesome home environment— the home I never experienced as a child. I was also very aware that someday I would need to face the issue of becoming a Christian. As a child, I had been taught by my grandmother and her church that God demands perfection. Even then, I knew that I could never live up to those standards. This misconception kept me from becoming a Christian all those years. Nevertheless, I was fully aware that it was something that I must do someday.

Now, in this small office I was forced to deal with this issue again. I had been asked by a man of faith if I was a

Christian, but I had to tell him that I was not. I explained my reason to him, but it made no sense to anyone but me. He quickly told me that I was way off base and gave me a little Bible tract to take home and read. The timing was perfect for this message to come to me. Because of financial pressures, I was at a point in my life where I was desperate for answers.

That night after my wife had gone to bed, I couldn't sleep. I found myself thinking about what my friend had told me and I began hearing his words over and over in my mind. I got out of bed, walked into the living room and found the Bible tract he had given to me. As I sat down and began reading, I discovered that none of us could do any amount of good things to earn our forgiveness and a pardon for the wrong that we have done. Our good deeds are as *"filthy rags"*, it said. I read that there were only two ways to go heaven. We could be perfect like God—live out our entire life and never make any mistakes...never sin. Oh well, so much for that one. I had blown it hundreds, even thousands, of times. I read on hoping that the other way would be something I could do.

It said there was only one person who had lived without mistakes—without sin; only one person had lived a perfect life. That person was Jesus. He had traded his own life, dying for us, so that those who believe and accept his sacrifice can enter paradise. Kneeling on my living room floor in the dark and all alone, I received Jesus Christ and became a Christian. It had been a long journey to get to this place, but I will have more to say about that later.

Oh.... hold on. Here comes another car. Again, my heart races and anxiety takes over because of the impending showdown. This confrontation was something that I never really wanted to happen, but to my sadness, it always did. One part of me longs for this one to be her. Lying there for hours, I felt that I knew why she had not come home. After all, this wasn't the first time I had to deal with the awful feelings of knowing that she chose to be in places and do things I could never accept. In my mind I saw this as her choosing these other things over her family, and that was always very hurtful. I also worried about her safety. My mind would wander from seeing her car overturned and lying there bleeding, to visualizing her on the dance floor of a nightclub in the arms of another. I could never begin to count the hours I spent having these thoughts and dealing with the emotions they brought with them.

Another false alarm and the room is totally dark again.

A New Lifestyle

Where was I? Oh yes, I had become a Christian. Well, I soon found a small church to attend and was baptized. We began going as a family, and we both became involved in various ministries. Many Sundays my daughter and I would go alone, and then on others, we appeared to be the textbook Christian family worshipping and serving together. We looked the part, too. I remember when my niece sent us a card saying how she hoped to someday have a life and family as perfect as ours. I wonder how many families in churches throughout the world are masquerading in the same way we were. Oh, I was happy with my newfound faith and happy that my family was following me. But I guess I knew that I was living in a fantasy world.

Square Peg ... Round Hole

Looking back, I realize I was trying to put someone who needed to be free into a cage. There was no way to contain her for long. From time to time, and when I least expected it, she would break out. And when she did, I would shame her, and she would crawl back into her cage with her head down as in defeat. The cage was an invisible one with bars made of my ideals of acceptable behavior. Down deep inside, I was terrified of the inevitable. I just knew the day would come when one of two things would happen, and both made me very anxious. First, she might possibly succumb to the guilt and conform to what I thought she should be—a perfect mother, wife, and church/lady. This bothered me because I didn't want to live with a robot; someone who lived only to please me. I wanted her to be what I wanted her to be because that is what she wanted as well. Does that make any sense? In other words, I wanted her to want to be what I wanted her to be.

My other concern was that she might completely rebel and fly away forever. This was my greatest fear, and one that caused me much worry. I was committed to this family and was determined that it would stay intact. For many years, I walked a tight rope trying to hold things together that, as it turned out, could never be. My dream was slowly fading right before my eyes, but I didn't want to give it up. Somehow, I just had to make this work and preserve my family.

I tried a lot of different things to save my marriage. A few times, I compromised my convictions by taking her places she wanted to go that I really didn't. Although I tried to enjoy myself, I had lost all desire for that kind of life. Then, I tried moving. As a last resort, I felt that if we moved to another state, far away from people who seemed determined to destroy our marriage, we just might make it work. I presented the proposed move, she consented, but when I began to prepare for the move, she changed her mind.

You Name It …

Have you ever known someone who just wouldn't give up? Once I was offered a job in south Florida. I took my family there, we looked around, and we met with the man I would be working for. On the way home, I asked if this is what she thought we should do. She thought about it and said yes. Within a few days, I was working there and preparing to move my family. After about six weeks,

I noticed that she seemed distant when I called her. This bothered me since we were hundreds of miles apart, and I couldn't sit with her to work things out as I had done so many times before. Finally, one night she told me she wouldn't be moving after all. I was shocked and asked why since, as a family, we had agreed to relocate. She said she wanted a divorce and that she "just didn't love me anymore." I called her every day and asked that she wait until I could come home so we could work things out. Then, I got the surprise of my life when she stopped accepting my collect calls. My own wife rejected my call, not once, but time after time. This was the deepest hurt and insult of all. To make it even worse, I wasn't able to speak with my daughter either. This was unbearable, and I had to do something about it at once.

Reluctantly, I called my employer telling him that I had some personal problems, and it would be necessary for me to go home. I also told him that I probably wouldn't be back. This decision was painful for me since it was the death of yet another dream. I had so hoped that my family could relocate and begin again. It seemed that the only chance for us was to start over in a new location with a resolve to make things work. Now, I was packing and headed back to what I thought was the source of all our problems.... our home. I have since realized that rarely do geographics cause or resolve deep-seeded problems in a relationship. The root cause is almost always the will or desires of one or both parties drawing them in opposite directions.

The weeks I spent in Florida without my family was special for me; I had renewed my walk with God and was humbled because of that. With few distractions in the evenings, I spent hours studying various passages of the Bible before going to bed each night. God had impressed upon me that in order to properly serve him and to live a life that would draw others to him, I must first be humbled. I looked at the lives of several men in scripture and saw this as the one common denominator of a successful servant of the King. Later, as I reflected on this time in my life, I understood why I was drawn to this focus of study. In the very near future, this newfound humility on my part would save my marriage yet one more time.

Finally, I arrived home. We had a few minutes of small talk and I quickly caught up on what my daughter had been doing. Then we sat at our kitchen table and I poured my heart out to her. I spent hours apologizing for everything I had ever done wrong and many things that I had nothing to do with. I took all of the blame for every problem we had in our marriage and told her that I would be a different man. I admitted that I had tried to mold her into the woman I thought she should be. I'm not sure why, other than the fact that God had been allowed to do a work in me, but that very afternoon she agreed to reconcile and decided to withdraw her demand for a divorce. For then at least, our family would remain in tact.

Reunited Once More

About that time, I heard the sound of kids laughing and the brakes of a school bus. It was Casey. My heart felt as though it would burst when I looked out the window and saw her get off and skip toward the house. We decided to play a little trick on her with my wife saying that I had not come home after all. She walked in the house and I could hear her ask, "Is Daddy home?" Wow! I couldn't believe that she wanted to see me so badly. Her mom told her no, and immediately she burst into tears. I ran into the room, grabbed her into my arms, and with tears rolling down my cheeks as well, I knew what I had done was worth it all. I was home now with my wonderful child.

Unfortunately, this wasn't to be the last crisis we would face. Others would follow, and every attempt to save my marriage would only be temporary. I continued to apply Band-Aids over a gaping wound, only to have them ripped off again. Some of the things I did caused improvements for a short time, but we soon found ourselves facing the same problems as before. I will admit that I was tenacious, and before long I would come up with another plan. Eventually, I discovered that marriage has to be a partnership, and if any plan is to be successful, both partners must participate.

Time for a Dilemma and a Decision

Here comes another car and the headlights seem brighter this time. The car is moving slowly and makes the appropriate turn onto our block. Then, I hear the sound that I have been waiting for all night. The tires of her car rolling over our gravel driveway make a loud crunching sound, especially at 2:00 am. Now I must decide how to respond to her and do it in seconds. Oh well, I decided to just play it by ear; that's what I always did. The problem was that every time this happened before, my playing it by ear resulted in a heated confrontation. I always regretted that when it was over and wished I could have dealt with it in a more productive way.

However, this time I did one thing different. Lying there for hours, I had made a decision that would set in motion circumstances that would change our lives forever. As I thought about our past and our current problems, I came to several conclusions. They were not profound, but nonetheless, I had finally accepted them and would act upon them.

First, we all make our own decisions as to how we live our lives, and I couldn't change anyone but myself. I tried to change someone who didn't want to change, and it wasn't working. Normally, if we have to force someone to do something, we will have to continue to force the person to keep doing it.

Second, I was trapped in an unhappy marriage that couldn't be fixed without divine intervention. I was a Christian who didn't believe in divorce, other than on grounds of abandonment, adultery, or possibly physical abuse. As committed as I was to keeping our family together, I needed some relief.

And finally, I would not go on being this miserable for another night. The only way I could do that was to just let go, trusting this whole matter to the Lord. I had tried everything conceivable. I had no more plans left. I resolved that I would be the best husband I knew how to be, but beyond that, I would rely totally on God, his guidance, and his wisdom.

To me, this was like taking on an impossible task at work. You don't want to admit that you can't do it, so you keep trying every approach imaginable. With each one, you become more hopeful that it will work this time and even begin to think of the rewards you will receive from your boss. Then, your plan collapses, and out of the rubble, you have to start over. Finally, after many tries, reality sets in and you decide that you cannot do this particular task alone. You call in one who can take over for you and make the best out of this very hard situation. There is some level of disappointment because you failed, but all of a sudden you experience total and complete relief from the stress of working so long on something you could never complete.

This is the way I felt that night when I recognized that, although I had previously seen it as my responsibility to make her happy, I had been trying to make it happen in my own way. So, I relinquished the task to God. Later I realized that even God would not force himself on her, but would allow her to choose her own path to seek happiness.

I must be honest and tell you that I allowed myself one last confrontation that night. But from that point on, I began doing things His way. He can take our life, in whatever condition, and begin to work out improvements and blessings far beyond anything we can conceive. As long as I thought I could solve all of my problems without him, using methods of my own design, the solutions never worked and I found myself back where I started. Because of my decision that night, I began a new life once again.

A New Start … Again

The next day, things began to get back to normal. We reconciled and went on with our lives once again until the next crisis. The difference was that I wasn't constantly in dread of that next time anymore. I had given my problem to the Lord—confident that he would guide and sustain me and enable me to work through each challenge in the very best way possible. I must say that as a result, I began to experience a measure of peace and happiness. I also began to learn a valuable lesson. Quoting a verse of scripture best summarizes this lesson:

"Trust in the Lord with all your heart and lean not on your own understanding. In all your ways acknowledge him and he shall direct your paths." Proverbs 3:5.

The word *paths* in this scripture took on a new meaning for me. It literally came to mean a road to my destiny. I am reminded of Israel's journey through the wilderness led by Moses. They knew they were headed for the promised land, but when you look at a map showing their route, you might think that they were driving under the influence. A trip that should have taken a few months, at the longest, took forty years. Why? Partly because they were being punished for their unfaithfulness to God, but also because there were lessons to be learned, and these lessons took time.

Little did I know that I was about to begin a new journey that would reshape my entire life. It would change who I was and where I was going. This new road would have very steep hills that would take every ounce of my strength to climb. It would also have deep, dark valleys where I would wonder if the journey would be worth the struggles. As I reflect on the road to my destiny, I can see how every layover served a purpose, and every bad experience prepared me to minister to someone else in the future. At a time in my life when I thought I should be relaxed and secure, there would come upheaval and turmoil. I would go from trying to live out my dream to surviving a nightmare.

Life is so very fragile. We think that we know where we are and where we are going. But then, the very next day, our whole world can be turned upside down, and we have no idea what will come next. But God can help us grow through each of these experiences if we learn to look to him for guidance.

Soon, I would need that divine guidance more than I could ever have imagined. I would have to learn to depend on God for everything and trust totally in his judgment. When I could not defend myself, I would learn to allow him to be my defense and shield. It would be an awesome adventure as I watched him work in the issues of my life. My future, and that of my daughter, would be in his hands and out of my control. What was most difficult to accept was that the dream that I had been clinging to for so long would have to be radically transformed. Out of it would come a destiny very different from anything I had ever envisioned.

Letting go of a lifelong dream can be very difficult. Most of us form images of what we want our lives to be. The problem is that many times we link ourselves with someone whose visions and dreams are very different from our own. I suspect that during the dating process, we share only small portions of these with our potential mate, while holding back quite a lot. Then, when we are married to that person, we may really open up and discover that our ideals are significantly different from those of the other person.

Conversely, what our spouse may feel is necessary to make his/her life happy and complete, may turn out to be not only quite different from what we desire, but even incompatible. It is here that the struggle begins as we seek to decide whose dream will we live out. "Surely the other person will understand that mine is best!" we think. But in reality, this is not at all likely. Thus the tug of war begins over what our life together will be like, and it may last for many years. Often, it develops into an all out war with everything that is most precious to us at stake.

2

The War Begins
When Allies Become Enemies

Because of the decision I had made, my whole way of thinking changed. For years, I had been under the bondage of insecurity in my relationship with my wife. Now, it felt like I was free for the first time in many years. No longer was I concerned about where she was or what she was doing. I knew that my daughter was always well cared for in my absence, since my wife loved her as much as I did. It also seemed as though we were getting along much better.

The economy was very bad in our area. As a result, I suffered a serious financial setback and decided to take some work out of town to try to recover. Soon, I was doing very well and sending a substantial amount of money home to liquidate our debts. We were living hundreds of miles apart, but spoke by telephone most every day. Occasionally, I would decide to take an unplanned trip home for the weekend thinking it would be a nice surprise.

My daughter was always so happy to see me. Once, I arrived very late on Friday night only to find a dim light in the living room, which turned out to be the television. I noticed there was no car in the driveway, and when I rang the doorbell, a young teenage girl who lived a few blocks away answered the door. She said that my daughter was sleeping and that my wife had gone out. Around midnight, she came in and instead of being happy to see me, she was very angry that I had not called to tell her that I was coming home.

This did not seem like normal behavior for a devoted wife who hadn't seen her husband in three weeks. I kept telling myself that it was just her way and that it probably upset her because it appeared that I still didn't trust her. After this happened several times, it began to become obvious that she had made her decision. Presented with my total trust, and with complete freedom to choose the life she would live, she had chosen the same things that had caused most of our problems in the first place.

It wasn't long after these incidents that she told me again that she wanted a divorce. Down deep inside, I guess I had known for several years that it would eventually come to this, but I still wasn't ready for those crushing words. I had never given up my dream of being married once and for a lifetime. What I was now witnessing was a marriage barely surviving on life support. The dream I had held onto for so long was in critical condition. It was only sustained at this point by a variety of tactics, which I employed in an effort to save our home yet once more. I tried courting her, I tried reasoning with her, and I even put my dignity aside by begging her not to destroy our family. As it turned out, all of these were futile and served no purpose. Her mind was made up, and this time it would not be changed.

Who Was That Masked Person?

There was nothing left for me to do but begin the process of trying to protect my daughter and myself. I hired an attorney who suggested that I also hire a private detective. I recommend that you never hire a detective until you are certain that you can properly handle what may be discovered. I wasn't even remotely prepared for what would be reported to me. It seemed that I had been living with someone whom I did not know. This person had somehow slipped into my life and taken the place of the wonderful woman I had fallen in love with seventeen years prior. That beautiful, sensitive and loyal woman with whom I had shared my life had vanished. Oh, how I longed for her to come back, but I was never to see her again. Instead, I was left to do battle with a complete stranger.

Without a doubt, one of the most difficult things I have ever done was telling my daughter that her life too would never be the same. I had hidden her mother's decision from her for several days, but because of impending legal matters, it became necessary to make her aware of this tragedy. I made one final plea with my wife as she put on her makeup and prepared to go out for the evening. My daughter was playing in her room and oblivious to what was about to take place. At that moment, she was a happy little ten-year-old girl completely secure with the life she loved so much. Unfortunately, that wasn't to last.

I walked into her room and closed the door. "Hey Daddy!" She hopped up on her bed and waited for me to come and play with her as I often did. I sat down beside her and began trying to explain something that made no sense to me. How could anyone expect her to understand at ten years of age?

When I told her that things would not be as they were before, she was devastated. She just began crying and screaming "No ... Daddy ...no!" Then she ran out of her room and into the dressing room pleading with her mother not to do this. I have thought about that moment for many years now, and wish there had been another way to tell her. I have finally decided that there is no good and proper way to tell a child that her life as she knew it is over. Even after all these years, I am still amazed when I see someone make a choice that is so selfish and unnecessary. A choice that does such incredible harm to so many people. I have never understood how a someone could want something so badly as to be willing to sacrifice the happiness of the children in order to have what that person seems to crave. Most people who have done this terrible thing will later realize that it wasn't worth it and will say that if they could go back, they would never do it again. But it seems to be something that, in the passion of the moment, cannot be resisted. I suppose that I feel so strongly about this because the very same thing happened to me as a teenager when my parents divorced.

Later that night, I had a private conversation with my daughter and told her that I loved her with all my heart. I wanted our family to remain intact but that just wasn't to be. I asked her who she wanted to live with and without hesitation, she said, "I'm living with you Daddy." I discussed this with my attorney, and taking his advice, the two of us moved out of our house very early one morning. Within a few weeks an emergency custody hearing was scheduled. The judge interviewed my daughter and she confirmed that she wanted to stay with me. After hearing the testimony of several character witnesses and my wife's attorney admitting that she was having an illicit relationship with another man, the judge granted me temporary custody. I remember thinking what a sad victory that was.

It Came out of Nowhere

Early during the separation, I bought a home in a nearby town where my mother lived. She agreed to move in with us and help take care of my daughter. After about two months, I was contacted through my attorney and told to have my daughter ready for visitation with her mother that weekend. That Friday she picked up my precious and happy little ten-year-old girl, but on Sunday afternoon, she brought back a withdrawn, sad, little stranger. Before that visit, my daughter was content to be with her new friends at school and church. After that visit, she spent most of her time in her room alone. I had no idea what had happened to cause her to change her so much. I only knew that my world had really begun to unravel yet once more. I was also to learn something new that would truly break my heart all over again.

My attorney called saying that he had learned from the opposing attorney that my daughter had changed her mind and wanted to live with her mother. She had not said anything to me about this and even despite her strange behavior, it still came as a total surprise. I felt that I had done everything humanly possible to give my daughter a home that was second only to the one she thought she had before the separation. I could not imagine that she would ever want to leave the wholesome environment that had been created for her and go back to nights with baby sitters and other problems. Heartbroken, I asked her about these new developments. Reluctantly, she admitted to her change of heart but would never give me a reason. Not only had my wife rejected me, but now also by my daughter.

Much sooner than I would have liked, it was time to go back to court for the divorce and permanent custody determination. My daughter, through her mother's attorney, asked to speak with the judge, and he allowed her, at ten years of age, to choose to move back with her mother. I can't remember ever feeling so low in my entire life. My dreams this time were truly shattered. The one person whom I loved more than I loved my own life was taken from me on Thanksgiving day. I felt that I had been swallowed up by injustice—abandoned by the one who was my main purpose for living. Emotions that I had never known before began to surface. Hurt that felt like the tearing of flesh filled my very being. The God whom I had trusted was nowhere to be found, and he was allowing me to suffer this alone. Where was he, and why was he allowing this to happen to me? So much for all that faith I thought I had. So much for his *"directing my paths."*

Part-time Dad

Now, all of a sudden, the tables were turned. I was the one cast out of the loop. I felt as though I had been betrayed yet again. Now I had to learn about something that I had feared for years. Because of experiencing several close encounters with separation and divorce, I had been forced to think about the possibility of becoming a non-custodial father and visitation with my child. It was a thought that caused anxiety every time it presented itself. Now it wasn't just a thought, it was a reality.

Now I was the one allowed to pick up my daughter every other Friday at 5:00 P.M. and take her back to her mother by 5:00 P.M. on Sunday. This inhumane, man-conceived, degrading, court-mandated means of allowing a non-custodial parent to spend time with a child was very difficult to adjust to. It was this visitation, however, that taught me how precious time really is. I savored every second, and all weekend I dreaded taking her back. I just knew there must be a better way to do this; one that wouldn't upset the lives of everyone involved—especially my child.

I once knew a lady physician who was divorcing her physician husband. They had two small girls, and the mother assumed that she would stay in the house with the children. The judge showed a true stroke of genius as he dealt with what was in the best interest of the children. The temporary custody ruling provided that the children would remain in the home they were familiar with and where they felt secure. The parents, however, would take turns living a week at a time in the home with the children. There were objections from both sides, but the judge did not give in. He said the children had not chosen the divorce and were innocent parties in the matter. It was the parents who could not get along and, as a result, were at fault. It would not be fair to punish the children by uprooting them every other weekend to go to a strange place to stay with the non-custodial parent. I thought about that decision and decided that it was the most brilliant ruling concerning custody and visitation that I have ever heard of. If this was the norm rather than the exception, I wonder how many divorces would be avoided.

The weekend visitations were like a very small slice of heaven. I missed my daughter so much for the two weeks we were apart. I would think every day about being with her for that oh so brief two-day weekend and would try to plan something special for her. Invariably, she would think of things she would rather do and off we would go. There was much goofy golf, movies, bowling, and more goofy golf. Sundays were my favorites. My daughter would always get up on her own and start getting ready for Sunday school and church. I was a very proud daddy with her at my side, and I'm sure it showed. She seldom attended church except when she was with me, but she really seemed to enjoy it when we went together. She spent time with the friends she made at church on the weekends she was with me. But more importantly, she was learning about Jesus and how to live the Christian life. That would be something that no one could ever take from her.

As for me, I was happy four days a month. The rest of the time I was sad, withdrawn, and angry. I was sad and in mourning due to the death of my dream. I had been so sure that I would be married once and for life. I thought we would raise our daughter, have beautiful grandchildren, and spend many wonderful years together in retirement. I was withdrawn and preferred not to talk to anyone who was happy and still living out his or her dream. It was depressing as I looked around and found many friends and family who seemed to be totally committed to their spouse and their life together. And I was very angry. I was angry at the wonderful person that I had married for disappearing on me. Where had she gone? Now there was only this woman who looked just like her, but definitely wasn't the same. The beautiful girl I married was intrigued with me, always wanted to be with me, and seemed passionately in love with me. How could she disappear and be replaced with this stranger?

I was angry at the legal system and the way it had failed me. I had been naive enough to think that the courts knew right from wrong and would make good decisions based upon moral and logical principles. Was I ever surprised to see that there are no guarantees for justice in our modern day court system! Scripture teaches that in the last days that which is right will be labeled as wrong, and that which is wrong will be accepted as right. It sure seemed to be that way in my case.

There were other issues in the divorce concerning property that I felt were grossly unjust. This was when I first asked the question "Why do bad things happen to good people?" You see, I really thought that I was a "good person." Oh, I knew what the Bible said: *"There is none good, no not one."* But I felt that I was really a good person, and I expected to be rewarded for being a faithful Christian father. I expected bad behavior to be punished and good behavior to be rewarded. However, I was experiencing just the opposite.

Troubled and in search of answers, I turned to the Bible. Somehow, I was drawn to the Psalms and found myself identifying with David as he cried out to God. I read Psalms 69 over and over where David says:

"Save me, O God; for the waters are come in unto my soul. I sink in deep mire, where there is no standing: I am come into deep waters where, the floods overflow me. I am weary of my crying: my throat is dried: mine eyes fail while I wait for my God."

I truly felt like I was drowning in a mixture of grief and despair. I felt helpless and for once, I had no answers. I kept reading...

"Deliver me out of the mire, and let me not sink; let me be delivered from them that hate me, and out of the deep waters."

Verse 17 summed up my feelings as it said,

"And hide not thy face from thy servant; for I am in trouble. Hear me speedily."

You see I really was in trouble, and I wanted God to show himself right then. As I saw it, he was being much too slow, and I needed help immediately. Well, God grew me a lot during those awful months, and now I see how he was working in my life when I thought he was on vacation. I don't remember when it was or where it happened, but the answer came one day when I least expected it. All this time I was expecting him to right the wrongs that I felt had been done to me. I knew he didn't approve of the injustice and the hurt I had experienced. Therefore, I had been waiting for him to do the obvious—turn the whole situation around and return my daughter to me. It didn't happen that way. In his still small voice he just said to me, "Let it go."

No! I Hate This too Much

"What? That's it? Let it go? Lord, you are God. You can fix this whole thing with one word or even one thought. Lord, I can't let it go!" And then, defiantly, I said, "If you won't do something, then I will!"

All these thoughts went through my mind in a matter of minutes. Certainly this could not be God's will for my life. Surely, there had to be a better way. If God would just sit down, think it over, he could figure it out! It took me quite a while, but gradually I began to remember who he is and who I am. He really does what is best for each one of his children—even when we can't see how these things can possibly be what are best. Finally I said, "OK Lord. I'll let it go. Thy will be done". It was then that I got that same feeling of relief and peace I had felt the night I was lying in bed waiting for my wife to come home. An overwhelming sense of his presence came over me, and I actually smiled. It wasn't just my problem anymore. He had taken the burden for me, and I came to realize that with his help this problem would be resolved in his way and in his time.

Imagine that you are in high school taking a final

exam in chemistry. Honestly, you know little more about this subject than you did the first day of school. You feel terrified because you know that you need to pass this test to graduate. None of the formulas make any sense to you and panic sets in. Suddenly, the teacher walks over and takes your test paper saying, "I have decided to take the test for you and give you whatever grade I earn." Can you just imagine the relief you would feel at having been given a way out? Just a few minutes prior you were overwhelmed with despair, but now you have a reprieve.

My Helper in a Time of Trouble

I cannot begin to imagine how I would ever have survived that darkest of all times without God. My heart bleeds for all those who don't know him, but most of all for those who experience the heartache of divorce and losing custody of their child without God's help. I kept thinking that if it was this hard with Christ in my life helping me, how could anyone make it through without him? He was my strength when I had none. He was my mighty counselor when all others failed. He picked me up and carried me when the justice system dropped and abandoned me. He gave me hope in a time of hopelessness.

That day I began my journey through this life all over again with a much lighter load. It certainly would not be the end of my troubles, and I would stumble many times in my faith. But I would never forget the lesson of this dark valley of my life. I would always remember the one of whom the Psalmist spoke in chapter 116:1-2:

"I love the Lord, because he hath heard my voice and my supplications. Because he hath inclined his ear unto me, therefore will I call upon him as long as I live."

I then resolved that now and forever, I would trust in him.

3

"K" Rations
When Life is Hard to Swallow

When I was just a kid, I remember overhearing some of the old timers talk about their days in the military. These men fought in World War II and served their country without hesitation. They discussed living in small tents, daily battles with mosquitoes, being wet, excessively cold or hot depending on the season, and other severe hardships they endured. They talked about being afraid when in battle with the enemy and their close brushes with death.

Ironically, there was one thing they all appeared to have in common. On the surface, we might think that it was trivial, yet they spoke of it as though it had been their most dreaded enemy. When they discussed it, they would grunt or groan and make a terrible face. Had it been some kind of high-powered gun used by the enemy? Was it a chemical or biological weapon that they feared so? You would never guess.

"K" rations was the name given to food supplied to the men for field training and battle conditions. Should they find themselves away from camp and cooking facilities, all they had to do was open their pack and choose from the canned or packaged food in their *"K" rations* kit. I once tried some while in the Boy Scouts, and it was without a doubt, the worst tasting food I have ever put in my mouth. One would have to be practically starved to want to eat *"K" rations*. These men had in fact eaten them on occasion, but I could tell that it had been a last resort.

There are circumstances that come our way in life which, like *"K" rations*, are also hard to swallow. A non-custodial parent is often starved for the attention of his child. He may go for two weeks or more without seeing his little one and is famished when the time finally comes. Quite often when he picks up his feast (his beloved child) on Friday, he may be disappointed. The child may not be responsive and may even be disinterested in activities the parent has planned. Many times few things turn out as the parent had planned, and by the time they part on Sunday, the parent has been left with a really bad taste in his mouth.

The one thing that kept him going for two long weeks has now left him depressed or frustrated. Sometimes anger will boil up as he thinks, "this just isn't fair." After the visitation is over, it may take several days to get over the negative feelings generated by this experience. Eventually, this may become a regular cycle, which begins with the excitement and anticipation of getting to see the child, followed by the frustration of watching another weekend visit go bad. Then, the final stage begins to develop— total and complete disappointment, which sparks feelings of depression. What can be done to break this awful cycle?

The Problem

It seems that children have a way of being brutally honest. I am sure you have witnessed a child noticing and speaking out bluntly about a physical peculiarity of someone. "Mommy! Look at the great big nose that man has." This can be most embarrassing for the parent who would like to just disappear when this happens. Likewise, children seldom make much effort to suppress their moods, likes, or dislikes. When they are happy, it shows; but when they are unhappy, everyone around them is unhappy too. They will usually make sure of it. In a two week period, a non-custodial parent has 48 hours to enjoy his children, teach them something, show how much they are loved, discipline them if necessary, and earn their respect. The custodial parent, on the other hand, has 288 hours to accomplish the same thing. I am reminded of the arcade game where you take a mallet and every time a head pops up, and you never know from which hole it will come next, you have to hit it with the mallet. The object is to hit as many as you can before time runs out. I'm sorry, but there just isn't enough time in a weekend to get a high score. This causes dad to feel like a failure and sometimes makes him wonder if it is even worth trying. I know this very well from my own experience. It may very well be for this reason that some dads do not press or exercise their right of child visitation, and he and his child begin to grow further and further apart.

It is here that many times a non-custodial parent reaches a crossroads in this process. It may be at this point that he realizes that remaining involved with his child may be the hardest work he has ever done. It is usually at this juncture that a decision must be made. Will this parent commit to never give up being involved in the life of the child even if that child rejects him? For you see, that is what it will take—a real commitment on the part of the parent. Unfortunately, it seems that far too many choose to take the easy way out here and simply begin to withdraw from their child's life. I realize that it is easier to do this than to stay in there while suffering hurt, rejection, and frequently depression.

This parent needs to realize that seldom does anything worthwhile happen to us without a considerable amount of effort. The greatest blessings and rewards we experience usually come after long periods of struggle. Maintaining a healthy parental relationship with our child through visitation is no different. We only have to decide which is more important: our present feelings, or what we can ultimately do for our child. I will speak more about this later on.

I also recognize that the custodial parent has difficult matters to deal with as well. Among these is the very hard task of doing the day-to-day job of a father and mother. This is extremely difficult and also unnatural. It was never meant to be this way. No one could ever take the place of a properly functioning in-house parent. Yet, many custodial parents are forced to try. I have been made aware of many situations where the non-custodial parent seems to have resigned from the life of the child. I personally know several wonderful moms who have begged these dads to become involved with their child again only to see no real response. Unfortunately, this happens much too often; however, there are also cases where the custodial parent plans events or arranges things so the child will not be available for a visit with the other parent.

Where anger and resentment persist, either parent, and sometimes both, may deliberately contrive ways to frustrate the efforts of the other as a way of "getting even." Sadly, the one who is really hurt by such schemes is the child. I would encourage both parents to make a very strong effort to view the visitation process from the eyes of the child, and thus do everything possible to make the arrangement work. It is especially important that the custodial parent does everything possible to keep the non-custodial parent involved in the child's life. This is assuming, of course, that there is no question of abuse or immoral activity around the child. This means setting aside anger and vindictive acts and rather thinking of the happiness and long term well being of the child. The court-mandated visitation arrangement is only a guideline, and in most cases, the child will benefit from spending more than the prescribed minimum time with the other parent. Both adults should make every effort to be flexible so that the non-custodial parent can flow in and out of the child's life much in the same way as when the family was intact.

Just Not Fair

There is another issue that is far too common and, when it occurs, can wreak havoc on the emotions of a divorced parent. Many times the non-custodial parent may be mostly or even completely to blame for the irreparable damage that has been done to the family. In those cases, perhaps justice has been served by having that parent removed from the family unit. In earlier years this was standard procedure in the court system. In the past two decades however, this has changed significantly and many times it is not the parent who is mostly to blame that is removed. There are far too many cases in which the non-custodial parent is not solely, or even mostly, to blame for what has happened to the family, and yet has been cast out. Many children are allowed to live with a parent who is displaying immoral behavior in the child's presence while putting selfish desires ahead of the child's welfare. Even though the parent's immoral behavior may be common knowledge...for example that parent may have a live-in lover...many times the judge does not see that as a detriment to the child. I would insist that this is always a problem.

If our society has come to the point where no one recognizes that type behavior as being wrong, then may God have mercy on us! It's here that it's only natural to be angry and frustrated at the injustice of the circumstances, which are, in many cases, prescribed by the courts. This is also a time when many of us question God. When what should be isn't, and what shouldn't be is, we find ourselves asking, "*Where is God? Why is he allowing this to happen?*"

Have you ever worked for a boss who did things that made no sense at all? He might have instructed you to do something that you knew was wrong or wouldn't work. You may have thought, "If I were in charge I would never ask anyone to do something so stupid." Have you ever looked at an interstate highway interchange that did a very poor job of facilitating the flow of traffic and wondered what the engineers were smoking when they designed that monstrosity? We often second-guess how people do things and we think, "I could have figured out a better way than that." As I pondered this subject, one Bible personality kept coming to mind. He was the one with whom I identified most at this particular time in my life. His name is Job.

Second-guessing God

The book of Job is fascinating in that it gives us a glimpse inside the spiritual dimension. It begins with the devising of a very strange cosmic test originating in heaven, yet one that would be staged on Earth. It depicts Satan asserting to God that the only reason people like Job lived good and faithful lives was because God had blessed them so abundantly and protected them from harm. God was actually very satisfied with Job's faithfulness and his right-eousness, so he put Job up as his entry in this unprece-dented contest. If you aren't familiar with the story you should read at least the first two chapters of the book of Job. In them you will discover how God agrees to allow Satan to afflict Job as they examine his response. And so the most terrible things happened to Job. His wealth was taken away, and his children and servants died, and his body becomes diseased and is covered with awful sores. Sometimes when I think I am in pain, I go to this book to see what Job had to deal with and always leave feeling that my suffering is not so bad after all. Amazingly though, Job was up to the challenge. He responded to the terrible things that happened to him by saying,

"*Naked I came from my mother's womb, and naked I will depart. The Lord giveth and the Lord has taken away; may the name of the Lord be praised.*" Verse 22 of Chapter 1 tells us, "*In all this, Job did not sin by charging God with wrong-doing.*"

The trials weren't over yet though. Seeing the miserable

condition of Job sitting in the sack cloth on a heap of ashes, scraping the wretched boils that were all over his body, and thinking that his situation was hopeless, his own wife told him that he should just *"curse God and die."* Three of his friends came to discuss his situation with him. They acknowledged that his life to outward appearance seemed blameless, but they went on to say that such bad things just do not happen to a truly innocent person. These things must be the result of some terrible hidden sin that he had committed. In answer to their accusations, Job speaks at length about life and suffering. He insists that he does not know why God is doing these terrible things to him but he continues insistently to maintain his innocence.

Have you ever questioned how God works and why he does what he does? Have you ever wondered why his timing is so different from our own? Have you thought about what you would do differently if you were God? Give it a try by finishing this statement:
"If were God, I would _____.
While you are thinking about your answer, I will give you mine.

"If I were God...
I wouldn't allow children to suffer.
I wouldn't send good people to hell.
I wouldn't allow bad people to get away with doing bad things.
I would have made the Bible easier to understand.
I wouldn't allow people to go hungry.
I wouldn't allow disease to kill innocent people.
I wouldn't allow wars to break out.
I wouldn't have made mosquitoes, gnats or horse flies.
I would speak out loudly so everyone could hear me (not in a "still small voice")
I wouldn't allow earthquakes, hurricanes, or torna-

does to injure people.
I would heal all of the sick people.
I wouldn't allow people to be lonely.
I wouldn't allow children to be taken from a parent
who loved them as much as I loved mine.

So, if I were God I would definitely do things differently—because I know best, don't you see?

If I had just had this conversation with God, what do you think he would have said? I think I know, what God would say. God would probably say just what he said to Job. He might ask me as he did Job,

"Where were you when I laid the foundations of the earth?"

I am sure He would put me in my place the way he did Job. Then, I would probably respond as Job did in Chapter 40 verses 4-5.

"I am unworthy— how can I reply to you? I put my hand over my mouth. I spoke once, but I have no answer—twice, but I will say no more."

I suppose it's only human for us to question God. When we lose a loved one, see a small child suffer and die, see an entire city destroyed by an earthquake, or see a parent separated from his or her precious child, we can't help but wonder why. When we see these things, we may question God, but when we look into his word, we are likely to be brought to the place Job was when God confronted him. In chapter 42 verses 2-3, Job says,

"I know that you can do all things; no plan of yours can be thwarted. You asked, 'Who is this that obscures my counsel without knowledge?' Surely I spoke of things I did not understand, things too wonderful for me to know."

Sometimes there are *"things too wonderful for us to know."* These are the very things with which we must trust to the God of our salvation. Therefore, I have come to this conclusion:

If I were God …I would not be a good one. And that makes me realize that I should be quite happy with the one that I have.

It May be Real but it Isn't Acceptable

Perhaps the one thing in my life that I found the hardest to understand was this; why would any parent ever do anything to risk destroying the family. In my situation, I could readily acknowledge that I had made many mistakes in my marriage. Like most or perhaps all people, I longed to be able to go back and relive certain moments of my life, so that I could change the way I conducted myself. At the same time I had to recognize that I really had tried very hard to keep my family together. I was always fearful that my family would become fragmented but I certainly never wanted my marriage to come to an end. I fought this with everything within me and was determined that I would keep the three of us together no matter how hard it might be. I was eventually to learn that this is something one person cannot do alone. It takes the sincere efforts of both partners. Lacking that, my family came apart, and I had my precious daughter taken from me. I was angry at the injustice of it and like those "*K rations,*" this whole situation left a very bad taste in my mouth.

Even though I had tried very hard to keep our family intact, I still had bouts with guilt and feelings of being a failure. I kept thinking that there must have been something more that I could have done to prevent this from happening to our family. I remember bringing my daughter home from the hospital as a newborn and holding her in my arms. I looked at her wrinkled little red face and her perfect lips and thought about how fragile and helpless she was. I was very aware that her life was in my hands as I held and cared for her. Thoughts of her growing up went through my mind, and I remember promising to always be there to protect her, teach her what she needed to know, and to love her. Now, I had lost control of her life and had been stripped of the privilege of performing my day to day responsibilities toward her. I began playing the "what if" game while putting together many different scenarios that I thought might have enabled my ex-wife to want to devote herself to her family. Unfortunately, this would only frustrate me more since we can't go back and change things in the past.

I finally had to accept the reality that things would never be the same. Now, my problem was to try to figure out how I could change this new situation I was in so that I could be more involved with my little girl and be the dad she needed so badly. I spent hours upon hours thinking as I drove, as I walked in the park, and as I worked at my job. I plotted and schemed coming up with off the wall ideas and plans that could never have been implemented. She deserved to have two parents intimately involved in her life, and I was faced with the reality that it could never be that way without living in the same home with her. I was living 60 miles away from her, having no idea what was going on in her life and I felt helpless. It seemed as though I was a father without a purpose, a father who had been abandoned.

4

Marooned
"Left Behind "

I heard some yelling and laughing outside and when I went to the window, I saw four kids playing in the street. I have always enjoyed watching children play, especially when they were not aware an adult was around. I am always fascinated by how imaginative they are and how quickly they can devise a game or a plan. These kids were no different. As I watched, they all suddenly began running down the hill. One ran out far ahead of the others and wasn't looking back. The others decided to play a trick on him and ducked behind some bushes. When he got to the bottom of the hill, he looked back and suddenly discovered that he was all alone.

It was at that very moment that I found myself feeling like that little boy at the bottom of the hill. All of a sudden the realization hit me and from that vantage point I had a new perspective seeing my situation very clearly.

What was I doing living in a town 60 miles from my daughter? It had seemed like a great idea when she and I moved there, since my mother would be available to help me take care of her. But now that she had been taken away from me, it no longer made sense. I worked in the same town where my daughter now lived, and I made the one-hour drive to work every day. In addition, when I had visitation, I made the same one-hour drive on Friday and again on Sunday. It became obvious that I needed to relocate, and that very day I decided to begin to do whatever was necessary to make that a reality.

It seemed that the first order of business would be to sell my home. However, a depressed real estate market would make it difficult to find a buyer for the house. Six months passed and the Realtor with whom I had listed the house still had not been able to find a buyer. I ran an ad in the local newspaper but had few calls and no real interest. I became discouraged and decided that I was stuck in this place and would never live close to my daughter again. Why was this happening to me?

As time seemed to creep by, I reconsidered my dilemma and decided once more that I must be closer to my daughter at whatever cost. I spent many hours thinking and wondering how I would get out of this trap that I had unknowingly set for myself. It was like being shipwrecked on an island with no way to get off. I felt that I was truly marooned. Finally, although it certainly was the last resort, I began advertising for a tenant to rent my house. The calls began coming in and before long, I had a signed lease. That next day, I rented an apartment about five miles from my daughter. It was an exciting time as I packed up to make the move that I had been praying would become a reality for so many months. Now I would be able to see her even through the week and call her whenever I wanted to. And she could call me, too. I felt very strongly that things would be better now. My hope had been renewed as I developed a new and fresh outlook for the future.

A Time for Reflection

The time that I had spent in that little town 60 miles away had not been completely wasted. It was the place of my birth and childhood, a place of so many memories. I spent many hours remembering my earlier years and the people who had impacted my life for both good and bad. It was a friendly place, and when I was growing up, everyone seemed to know everyone. I remember not liking that much at the time. It was as if no one had any privacy and far too many people knew our family business. Now, looking back, I see that mostly as something to be desired.

The whole town was a bit like a very large family. People helped each other and really seemed to care most of the time. Thomas Wolf was right, though, when he said that you can't go home again. Nothing was the same and it never would be. Most of my extended family lived there, and during my time there, I had renewed my relationship with them. I also became active in a warm and loving church where I had been asked to teach a college and career Sunday school class. I made a few new friends and because of the slow pace there, I had plenty of time to reflect on my life and my circumstances. All of this had been great, but without my daughter I knew that I could never be completely happy there. Now, I was going home again—my real home—or at least five miles from it. As the saying goes, "The home is where the heart is" and my heart was wherever my daughter was.

It seemed as though I had been starting over on a monthly basis since my daughter and I first moved out of what had been our home. There was one dilemma, one emergency, one life changing surprise after another. With each one, I was forced to adjust and regroup, forced to redirect my energy time after time. This move was just another one, and I felt as though I was up to the challenge. I had selected an apartment that was within my budget and rented a moving van. As I was loaded the van, I wondered how many more times I would move before things settled down. Of course, I had no idea. I remember thinking that there is something emasculating about a forty-plus year old man in a rented moving van—moving potted plants, shower curtains, and everything else he owns from his own nice house into a rented apartment. This wasn't what I had expected when years earlier I had thought about my up-coming middle-age crisis.

I was beginning to learn yet another lesson and that was to hang on to things … *loosely*. For some unknown reason we have a tendency to get very attached to the things around us. We especially cling to items that give us our identity, which of course, we ALL desperately need. The collection of things that we really need to get by in this world is very small in comparison to what we tend to accumulate and think we must have.

When I was a young boy playing with my friends, we would often build a fort from sticks, old lumber, straw and anything else we could salvage. Then, we would get into the fort and dare other kids who were not a part of our army to attack us. That pitiful little fort made from trash somehow made us feel safe and secure. We were John Wayne and Randolph Scott, and no one could touch us. As we look around at the things we have collected over the years, most of it is worth very little from a monetary standpoint. Its true value comes from the way it makes us feel. We have accumulated these things over time, and in the process, many of them seem to have been molded into what forms our identify. We think that if we lose them, we may cease being the person we have become. As I loaded that van, I looked at the items that I called mine and thought to myself: If this is who I am, then I need to create a new identity. So many pots and pans and I didn't even know how to cook.

A Life in a Box

This experience caused me to recall one of the saddest days of my life that had taken place several years earlier. My father and I had grown quite close in those final years of his life and my heart was broken by his sudden death. The days between his death and his funeral were naturally very emotional and quite draining.

A week or so after the funeral, my sisters and I decided to meet and go through our father's house dividing his personal effects. There was so little that it took only a short time. As we were about to leave, we saw a small box that he had put up in an out of the way place. We took it down, opened it, and began to examine its contents. After only a few minutes, it had become apparent that this little box contained things that were special to him.

There was a very old letter from a friend that I never knew he had. It was cordial with just small talk and a statement at the end about how much my dad's friendship had meant over the years. I pulled out a program of a Junior Miss pageant that I remember him attending. There, printed in the list of contestants was the name of one of his granddaughters. A key chain, a few business cards, some phone numbers of people in other cities from another era of his life—all meant little or nothing to his children but apparently had meant a lot to him.

What we had been looking at was his life in a box. Had he ever thought that someday, his children would be going through these things? Had he left us clues to secrets that he had clung on to for so many years? Probably not. These were just mementos of days gone by. These were a means by which he could revisit the good times; the times he had enjoyed and the people who had passed through his life bringing him happiness.

As I think back on this experience, I marvel that such a small box could contain the things that defined my dad's life. What size box will I have and what will it hold? His life had consisted of sixty-three years, and a heart attack had brought it to an abrupt end. This experience has caused me to think many times since about the day when my daughter will be sorting through those things that were important and special to me. Some of these are the wonderful cards sent to me by people who are much more thoughtful than I am. Though I probably never even acknowledged receiving most of them, they brought me great happiness and for even a brief moment, made me feel significant. There is a very old pocketknife that belonged to my grandfather who was my hero. My daughter will also find everything she has ever written to me, every little drawing she did in church or elementary school that I was able to save. There will be those photographs that are most special to me. Most will be of my little girl and her very proud dad doing some fun and silly things together.

When we sort through all the "things" of our lives, the truth is that we can reduce those that are most important to a small box. The contents of that small box will speak volumes about where we are focusing our attention now. As my daughter closes up my little box and walks out the door, I would like for her to have seen in its contents a dad who loved her dearly, who walked faithfully with his Lord, and who cherished his relationships with others. I pray that this will be my life in a box.

Here I Go Again

I was finally settled in my new place and to my surprise, living in the apartment was kind of nice. There was no yard to keep up, no house to maintain, and since it was a small two-bedroom apartment, it wouldn't take much effort to keep it clean. Best of all, I was just three minutes from work. After I was all moved in and had things somewhat in order, I sat down and finally relaxed. I began to think of how different things would be now. Surely I would become a greater part of Casey's life and re-take my role as her father. I reached for the phone and called to tell her that I had moved in and would pick her up Friday to spend the weekend with me. She really seemed excited and happy that I was close by again. Everything would be better now—I just knew that it would. I was still clinging to hopes of her coming back to live with me again. I wanted to do everything I could to make her feel at home with me and happy to be more a part of my life.

I realize now that I lived in denial for several years. Just when I would get a taste of reality, the fact that she would never permanently live with me again, I would somehow convince myself that somehow, someday she would change her mind and come back to me. I could make a new home with just my daughter and me, and she would be happier than ever.

Are you a non-custodial parent and currently denying what is real? I am not saying that you should give up your hope of becoming reunited with your child. What I am saying is that there comes a time, and believe me the sooner the better, when you should prepare yourself to live alone. What I eventually learned as I accepted the fact that I would be living alone, is that there is a vast difference between aloneness and loneliness. You can be alone and yet not be lonely. If we are depending on our child to fill a void that is causing us to be lonely, anything we can realistically expect the child to do for us will be at best a temporary fix. Children eventually grow up and move out, or at least they should, and then what will we do? This is something that both the custodial and the non-custodial parents must face. But this is a time that can be productive and spent learning how to be a whole person without others in your life.

There is one catch though. I don't believe that it can be completely, successfully done without God. There will always be a void… a missing link, when we choose to leave him out of our life. He is our creator, and he above all is truly the *"Lover of our soul."* The reason that he chose to allow us to exist is that we might come to recognize who he is, glorify him, and be drawn into fellowship with him.

I only wish that I had known these things earlier. For a very long time, I was depending on an innocent little girl to fill a void in my life. I can assure you that I missed her so much it hurt. But, the void wasn't hers; it was God's. I had gone off and left him while chasing my daughter. I had put my need to be with her far ahead of his need to be with me. In the name of being the perfect father, I had abandoned my perfect Father. You see, there should never be anything or anyone who means more to us than God. How it must hurt him when we leave to chase after someone or something else. He deserves our very best and our total devotion. As you deal with the difficult issues of your life, remember that he feels too. He longs to be with his child (you) more than we can ever imagine.

As I think back, I had been marooned in a town sixty miles from home. My daughter and I had gone there together, but she left me and went back to the only home she had ever really known. Like the little boy running down the hill, I had looked back and found myself all alone. But now, I had managed to get off that little island where I had felt marooned and had moved very close to her again. So many miles no longer separated us; no longer would I feel like an outsider. I knew that things could never be the way they were when she was younger, but I would do whatever I could to get back as much as possible of what I had lost. Also, I would be able to do a better job of fulfilling the vow I made to her when she was a newborn. I would be there for her whenever she needed me, and I really needed her to need me.

I can't imagine what it would be like to not have my daughter. I would be lost. From her birth, she has given me purpose and a reason to be. I love her tender heart and the way things can make her cry when you least expect it. I love her zest for life and the way she laughs at her own mistakes. She is also a caring person. Once when she was in the second grade, she came home and told me about a little girl that she was spending time with on the playground. She was so happy and shared how she had told the little girl all about Jesus and had led her in a prayer to become a Christian. I remember tears welling up in my eyes as I saw how special she was. I was truly blessed above all men. Giving her up, was out of the question and I would fight for every moment she might give me.

Only the Lonely

Well, at least I was right about one thing. Living close to work sure was nice. Because of this I was able to sleep an hour later in the morning and drive the one and one-half miles to work in minutes. Also, my apartment was on the beach and I enjoyed my long nightly walks. The sound of the waves and the cool breeze on my face were very soothing—even therapeutic. Only one thing could have make it better. But, she was always doing homework or going somewhere with her friends. I never knew a little girl her age could be so busy. Nevertheless, I was close by again and if she needed me, I was just a few minutes away.

Although it was nice not having a lot of lawn work and such, there was one problem with this new setting. I soon found that I had far too much time on my hands. I had resigned my teaching duties at the church I attended before I moved, and was now looking for a church to attend in my new location. Also, since I was so close to work, that gave me two extra hours each day to fill. I began jogging but still found myself sitting in the apartment for hours each evening reading or watching television. Since there was little worthwhile to fill my time, I would usually think far too much. At this point in the process of healing from a broken marriage and separation from my daughter, too many hours spent thinking was not a good thing. I began to revisit all of those same emotions and the "pity parties" began once more. Loneliness was something that had become a far too frequent visitor.

Once many years ago, I was traveling home from out of town with a friend. He was driving his car and suddenly it just stopped. The engine was not running, there were no lights, no power, nothing. We coasted to a stop on the interstate at an interchange. After checking under the hood, we decided that we needed to go for help. In a few short minutes, we were out of sight of the interstate walking down a very dark road and looking for help. I can honestly say that I have never experienced darkness like that before or since. I remember dragging my feet on the asphalt in order to know that I was still on the road. I could feel my pupils dilating to the point that they almost hurt.

Loneliness can be like that darkness. It can well up in us very quickly and seem overpowering. It's when we are this lonely that sometimes we get desperate. We may feel that we have nothing to lose since we are so miserable. "I would rather be with the wrong person than be alone," you might think. What we need to realize is that "loneliness is potentially destructive, while aloneness can be productive. The secret is to turn our loneliness into aloneness because aloneness is manageable.

As a young teen, I came to know a man who had spent many years living in a large city. He had made the serious mistake of getting into a fight and killing another man. After serving his time, he decided that he would look for a place where he could be alone for the rest of his life. He moved to a river swamp in south Mississippi, bought a small boat, and started fishing for a living. He was happiest when he was alone traveling up and down the river checking his trotlines. We became close friends since I was just a kid and no real threat to him. He taught me all about the river, hunting, fishing, but more than that, he taught me a lot about being alone. He was never lonely but was alone much of the time.

It was while I was spending so much time alone in my new apartment that I remembered this man. I recalled that I never heard him complain about not having people around. I had never seen a sad look on his face, and never once saw any emotion that resembled loneliness. Then I remembered the way he lived his life. His home was a small one-room cabin with only the bare essentials. When he needed to go to the store or into town for any reason, he just asked someone to take him since he didn't own a car. He had a dog that was with him everywhere he went, even in the boat on the river. He regarded money as a necessary evil and only needed it to purchase the basic necessities.

After thinking about these things, all of a sudden it hit me and I discovered his secret to being content to live alone. He was always helping other people with anything they needed. He would take someone fishing who knew nothing about it and teach him how to catch fish. He would help repair someone's outboard motor or leaky boat. He was always giving fish away that he had caught to sell and game that he had killed hunting.

He was a giver and as a result, had a network of people who were genuinely grateful to him. They were always bringing him things they thought he might need or like. I remember once all the ladies in the group of nearby camps decided to redecorate his little house. They gave me the responsibility of creating a diversion for about an hour while they did their work. I thought of some reason for the two of us to go for a boat ride up the river. When we came back, he walked into his house, looked around as the ladies yelled, "surprise," and for the first time since I had known him, I saw tears roll down his cheeks. They had made curtains, bought him a new bedspread, put new place mats on the table, and a nice rug on the floor. He was truly overwhelmed and grateful, and they were delighted too.

He was content with his aloneness because he had invested his time and efforts in others. Fortunately, when we do that, we always get something in return. We get a feeling of satisfaction and purpose when we do something for someone else. We also usually get gratitude, reciprocal acts of kindness, and love in return. This goes a long way in filling whatever void might be in our life that brings on feelings of loneliness. During the week most of the camps were unoccupied and he was alone, but he wasn't lonely. He had his memories to keep him company, memories of both his kind deeds and theirs also.

In my life, I have learned that being alone can be a blessing or a curse. It depends on what we do with it. I have experienced incredible blessings from God while alone...with him. Had someone been there with me, it just couldn't have happened. In solitude, thoughts have come to mind that turned out to be solutions to problems. Again, with someone around monopolizing my time and

conversation, the problems may not have been solved. In Mark 6:31, Jesus tells the apostles,
"Come ye yourselves apart into a desert place, and rest a while."

This may have been his way of telling them that sometimes they needed to be alone. Aloneness is something to be appreciated, to be managed, but also to be enjoyed in moderation. You see, there is a time for everything and certainly a time to be with others. Nevertheless, to be alone can be an opportunity to experience untold blessings. I eventually learned to be alone without being lonely, and it changed my life.

I'm Right Here Casey

I suppose that was a good thing since it was also about this time that Casey began making excuses when my weekend would come. At first I was very rigid and told her that it wasn't her choice. I would tell her that I had not seen her for two weeks and she **WAS** coming to my place this weekend. Well, she usually complied and seemed to try to make the best of it. But her reluctance continued to occur and I was faced with a choice. Would I force the issue and make her come stay with me against her will? What would that accomplish? I was afraid that it might cause her to resent me and never want to be with me. My other choice was to allow her to decide when she would come to stay with me. The danger here was that if the choice was hers, she might never choose to be with me. That would destroy me for sure. Could I take that chance? This can be a real dilemma for non-custodial parents, and the perfect situation to make some very serious mistakes. However, the child must never doubt that you want her or him with you. Regardless of whether or not it is possible to be with them, it must be clear to children that you are completely committed to being their parent first. This may mean giving up your job, future opposite sex relationships, your hobbies, and everything else should it be necessary, in order to be with them . No one is more important, and they have to know that. It means everything to them.

"Hi Casey, it's Daddy. I just wanted to make sure you still want me to pick you up tomorrow at 5:30. I hope you have been thinking about what you would like to do." I held my breath hoping for a positive response. It wasn't to be. "Oh Daddy, I meant to call you yesterday. I have been invited to go to Gulf Shores with Jenny and her family for the weekend, and you know how I love the beach and swimming pools. Do you mind Daddy? I will stay with you next weekend.... I promise."

I was five miles from her but it seemed like five hundred. I remember thinking, "If I had six kids, would there be at least one of them that would want to be with me?" What was wrong with me? I felt like I was trying so hard to be a good dad to her, but the harder I tried, the less of her time I seemed get. I spent countless hours, day after day trying to figure out what I could do differently that would change things. What could make her want to be with me that I had not already tried? Surely there was something that I could do or say that would bring her back to me again.

"OK Baby. Go ahead and I will see you next weekend. Be careful and have fun. I love you." Not what I really wanted to say, but what good would it have done to do otherwise. It would only have ruined her weekend. Yeah, well, at least I lived close to her now. I suppose I did the right thing, at least I hope so. Only time would tell.

5

I'm Dreaming
of a Past Christmas
You Can't Take it Back

Christmas around our house had always been very special. From the time Casey was two, we looked forward to seeing the delight on her face when she got up and went to the tree that special morning each year. As she grew older, she would usually wake up before her mom and me and run into our room. "Mom! Dad! Can we go to the tree now and see what Santa brought?" Oh, that was priceless! Here she was in her little faded blue silk gown walking around on her tiptoes or jumping up in bed and begging us to get up. Then we would all go together down the hall and into the living room. My wife always decorated a beautiful tree, and there were lots of gifts, most of which were for Casey. These were the best of times, and I had felt sure that it would always be this way.

Several years had passed now since those wonderful Christmas mornings, and nothing was the same. The small apartment certainly wasn't the warmly decorated home of my daughter's early childhood. Christmas shopping this year was extremely difficult for me. I couldn't seem to decide what to get her no matter how hard I tried. Finally, after days of agonizing over various ideas, I settled on what I thought would be the perfect gift for her along with several other smaller items. It's ironic that now, I can't for the life of me remember what it was and I suppose that it doesn't matter. What I do remember very vividly was her reaction when I gave it to her.

I woke up on that Christmas morning very excited

about what that day would hold. First, I would get to pick up my daughter around ten and bring her back to my apartment to open her gifts. Then we would go out of town to spend the day with my family. She always loved seeing her cousins and aunts, and I was certain that it would be a very good day. I called to tell her I was leaving my place and would pick her up in fifteen minutes. She was extremely eager and asked that I hurry. This only made me feel even better about what was in store. She was probably eleven years old and certainly still a little girl in my eyes. When we got back to my apartment she could not wait to open her gifts. I insisted that she open the lesser gifts first saving the "big" one for last. Finally, it was time and I watched her closely as she ripped the paper off. The expression on her face gave away her disappointment though she tried very hard to act pleased. She had wanted a bicycle and had told me so. I wanted to get her something that was my idea. I wanted it to be special and a surprise.

There are a few events in my life that stand out as times when I really blew it. This was very likely my greatest failure of all as a parent. The months of frustration, the hurt, the gross injustice, having been forced to relocate twice, being separated from her, and on and on all culminated in this one moment. She was not the only one at that moment that was disappointed, so was I. But worse than that, I was infuriated at her. At that point, I really lost it...and with an eleven-year-old child...and **ON CHRISTMAS MORNING**! This was certainly one of those moments I would give anything to be able to go back and to change my reaction. If only I could just correct the wrong that I did on that day. I said a lot of mean things. I told her that she never wanted to see me. I told her that nothing I ever did was good enough for her, and that she had chosen her mother over me. Then I really did a dumb thing. I said, "Why don't I really make you happy and just take you back home?"

By this time, she was crying and saying that was just what she wanted. I took her home and went back to my apartment where I prayed to die. Well, that prayer was not answered and I gradually realized that I would have to live with the memory of my behavior for the rest of my life. This wasn't really me; it was the monster of my emotions raging out of control. It was as if I had transformed from this nice little daddy-type person into the "Incredible Hulk" in a matter of seconds. I think that one way that I might have avoided this would have been to think through all of the possible scenarios before it happened so that I could have been prepared. If I had been able to anticipate what her reaction might be in case she didn't like what I gave her, perhaps I could have been more understanding when it happened. All I can say is that I didn't and for that, I am really sorry.

Make Yourself at Home ... Please

That seemed to be a turning point in our relationship. A few months later, I bought a fixer-upper house, remodeled it and moved into it. Now I was even closer to her; probably three miles or so. I had allowed her to participate in decorating her room and I tried to make it just the way she wanted. She was enthusiastic while the decorating was underway, but soon afterwards, she lost interest in this new environment.

From the very beginning of my weekend visitation with her, there was one thing I noticed when she came to my house. It was the same every place I had lived. Maybe it was a small thing to some, but to me it was something that bothered me immensely. I noticed that she never unpacked. She lived out of her travel bag. She would just pull out what she needed as she needed it and leave her things in her bag. There were times when she might be outside doing something with a friend and I would have this strong urge to go into her room and empty that bag, iron all of her clothes, and hang them up. I never did that but neither did she. I have thought about that for many years and I have finally come to a conclusion. It wasn't so much that she never unpacked her clothes, but rather that she never mentally unpacked. She always acted as if she was just visiting and never as if she really was at home.

There's an old story that I just love about an old ninety-year-old grandpa. His grandson had taken flying lessons and passed his test receiving his license. For months he had been asking his grandfather to go up with him. The standard response was "I've lived ninety years with my feet on the ground and that's the way I will die." But the grandson would not give up, and finally the grandfather gave in. They arrived at the airport, got into the plane and grandfather was strapped in. They took off and climbed to three thousand feet. Then they circled back, made an approach and landed flawlessly. The grandson helped his grandfather out of the plane and as they were walking back to the car he said, "Well Grandpa, how did you like it?" "Oh I guess it was all right," Grandfather said. "But I want you to know that I never did put my full weight down."

Well, neither did my daughter. Did you ever have company and they wouldn't take off their coats? That tells us that the visit is only for a short time and they will be leaving soon. My daughter's bag with her things still in it spoke very loudly to me. It said she did not consider this her home and I was to finally realize that she never would. She knew that she was just there on a short visit and soon would be returning to her real home. I always resented that. Somehow I expected this little girl to shift gears when she arrived at my place and completely accept what I had attempted to create for her. I thought that she should be able to forget about her room back at her mom's where all her possessions were. The instant she arrived, she should be thrilled to be here in this strange place. She surely should unpack and relax, and "put her full weight down." What was wrong with this kid?

I have come to finally understand that there was nothing wrong with her. Absolutely nothing! I used to hear a mom or dad talking about being so frustrated at the behavior of their child. One might say of their two-year-old, "All he wants to do is go all over the house and drag out anything that isn't nailed down." Another couple would say of their eight-year-old little boy, "I can't get the kid to come inside. He would live in the back yard in a cardboard box if I would let him." My standard response would be, "The very idea! He's acting J U S T   L I K E an eight-year-old." My daughter was acting just like a twelve-year-old girl. The very idea! Didn't she know she was supposed to conduct herself like a twenty-five-year-old woman?

What was I thinking? Why did I expect so much of this innocent child? Truthfully, I wasn't thinking ... at least not of her. I was thinking of myself and that was all. Oh, I did all the things I could to make her feel comfortable and at home. But I really did those things so she would be pleased—which is what it would take to please me. I wanted to be happy at all cost and I was depending on her to make that happen. After all, she was all I had left now, and it was up to her restore at least a little bit of what I had lost. She had a tough job on her hands but somehow I thought she was up to it.

There would come a time when I would realize that she couldn't create an environment that would bring happiness into my life. She could never make things "normal" again. There is nothing "normal" about a broken home. Our family had become fragmented and dysfunctional. Socially, it seemed as though I didn't fit in anywhere anymore. All of my friends were married and when I was with them, I was always like a "third wheel." In church, there seemed to be married couples everywhere I looked. The church programs were geared to the traditional family and I felt like the little runt kid running around the huddle trying to break in somewhere.

He Leadeth Me

After my second move, I began to look for a new church home. I was searching for a place where I could get involved and would be accepted in spite of the "divorced" label that I now wore. Soon, I was joining such a church even though there were no specific programs for single adults. But the people there didn't seem to focus on a person's marital status. I soon began teaching a Bible study class and got involved in youth ministry. I was building relationships with the youth and the other workers. This caused me to remember something I had learned a few years earlier. We are most miserable when we are focused on our needs and the things that we don't have. We are happiest when we involve ourselves in the lives and needs of others.

Even today, when I start feeling a little down or sorry for myself, I immediately think: "OK...it's time to stop dwelling on my own problems and start finding ways to help others with theirs." As my focus changes from my needs to the needs of others, I begin feeling much better. I encourage people whenever I can to broaden their horizons as they reach out to others. We are at our very best when we find our true purpose in life. We can often do this by figuring out what we can do best. This became a reality in my life when I moved from working with youth to working with single adults.

At my new church home, I was treated very well and allowed to serve in several areas. But as kind and gracious as the people were to me, I was single again and they weren't. I wanted a place where I could be with others who had been through divorce; others who lived alone like me and with whom I could build friendships. After working with youth for five years, I finally saw an opportunity to start a single adult ministry. I began teaching a Sunday morning Bible study class and soon we were planning social activities as a group. It was here that I could empathize with others who had experienced divorce. I was able to listen and give input to persons who were very lonely. They were very helpful to me in many ways as well. When a person would tear up while talking about missing his child, I knew just how he felt. So many issues that these divorced people faced, I had already experienced. I was standing on the other side and in at least some cases, could help them across.

A few years later, I was impressed to start a divorce recovery program in our church. This was by far the most rewarding ministry I had ever been involved in. On the first night as they came and registered, in many cases I could see the hurt in their eyes. Many would come beaten down and with little or no hope left in them. Often, by the third week, I was able to see them begin to heal and watch as their hope was restored. I saw many who had withdrawn to the safety of their homes begin to come out and join in the social events connected to our singles ministry. Yes, there is life after divorce, and this program would show many how good that life really could be.

It was at this church that was reunited with an old acquaintance from years back. The first time I walked into the sanctuary, I saw him standing at the door ushering. I must admit that I was taken aback since the last time I had seen Wallace, he was anything but a church usher. The following week, our paths began to cross and we would run into each other at the oddest places. Finally, we had lunch and talked over old times. It seems that he had become a Christian about the same time that I had. There had been a radical transformation in his life and family. We soon became friends and I was frequently spending time with him and his family.

Looking back, I can't for the life of me understand why these wonderful people would reach out to me the way they did. I had nothing to offer them and due to what I had been through during the previous years, I couldn't have been very good company. Nevertheless, they literally took me into their family. They would call me and ask if I would like to go out to dinner with them. On Sunday, I might be invited to their home for lunch. Wallace and I purchased a property together and resold it. Then we found another and another and before long, we were partners in several ventures. I know now that God makes every provision that is necessary for his children. He surely made one that was vital to my life when he gave me these wonderful friends. They are still an important part of my life even today.

The Promised Land

It was due to my friendship and partnership with Wallace that I came to own the property where I would make my home and finally settle down. He called me one day and said that we needed to look at 240 acres located less than two miles from our church. I couldn't imagine that there would be that much land for sale so close in. As we drove over it, I remember thinking how ugly it was. The timber had been cut about a year earlier and there were piles of limbs and debris everywhere. As we wondered what we could do with it should we decide to purchase the property, we were also a little intimidated by the price. We decided to take the matter to God and trust him for the answer to our dilemma.

It was only about a week later that we entered into an agreement to purchase the property. We obtained financing and before I knew it, we were its new owners. Over the next several months, we sold 60 acres for subdivision and 80 acres to an individual for a home site. Wallace and I decided to divide the rest, and I received one of the greatest gifts the Lord would ever give to me. My portion consisted of 55 acres located both on a beautiful deep-water creek and a large lake. There was a five-acre island with a 50-foot wide natural land bridge connecting it to my other property. I was also to enjoy a beautiful sandbar on the creek for many years to come.

I decided to build a large barn with a loft that became

my home. I had begun the cleanup months earlier and the beauty of the property was slowly revealed. It was here that I learned about the provisions that God makes for His children. He had gifted me with a place of incredible beauty and serenity. It was a sanctuary that he had prepared for me, and to the best of my knowledge, I was the first person to ever make it home. I would spend hundreds of hours cleaning up, planting grass, mowing, building structures, improving roads and planting flowers and plants. But I would also spend as many hours walking, looking and enjoying its beauty. I was truly able to be alone with God there and as a result, my walk with him was enhanced greatly. It was also to become a place that would be used in my ministry to single adults. We have had many wonderful times together there cooking out, riding four-wheelers and jet skis—just relaxing and getting to know each other better.

I have also sensed that this was God's way of replacing the losses resulting from an unjust court decision during my divorce. Not only did he make the replacement, but also it was multiplied ten-fold. It was during one of those walks on my property that I was reminded of when I was raging over the injustice that had been hurled upon me and he had told me to *"Let it go"*. It wasn't something that I wanted to do, but nevertheless, I did let it go. Now, I have been so greatly blessed and often marvel at what God has raised up from the ruins of my earlier life. Surely,

"Thy mercy, O Lord, is in the heavens; and thy faithfulness reacheth the clouds." —(Psalms 36:5)

Oh by the way, just another word about that awful Christmas that I was so ashamed of. In recent years I have discussed it with my daughter and told her how sorry I was for the way that I behaved. I got the surprise of my life when she told me that she couldn't even remember that it had happened? Boy, do I feel stupid! I grieved for years over this and she didn't remember it. Kids are miracle creatures. At least mine is. (And very gracious too, I suspect.)

6

We were Dysfunctional when Dysfunctional wasn't Cool
A Childhood Revisited

Earlier I mentioned that the reason I was so determined to have an intact and functional home is that I had never experienced that as a child myself. The impact that this had on me was powerful and shaped my thinking about how parents should conduct themselves and what factors are necessary to make up a healthy environment in which to raise a child. In an effort to better explain my feelings about parent-child relationships, I will share some of my childhood experiences.

My earliest memories of my parents were of drinking, dancing, bars and fighting. Later, though, things got better. They gave up dancing. For many of my younger years, I really thought the life we lived was normal. I was the youngest of three children and usually got special treatment. I didn't get nearly as many beatings as my two older sisters. Friday and Saturday nights were always very special for our family. We would all get cleaned up, dressed and the whole family would load up in the car to go some place real nice. The first stop was the movies. Here my parents would drop off my two sisters to enjoy a double feature. Then, my mom, dad and I were off for a great night out.

Our destination was usually one of about three places and a lot of my parent's friends would always be there. We would walk into a dark smoke-filled room that smelled of stale beer. I can still hear the loud talking, the laughter and those country music songs that had become so familiar to me. Everyone would say hello to my mom and dad and someone would reach down to pinch me on the cheek and say, "You are a cute little fellow. " I loved looking at the lighted beer signs and especially the jukebox with the pretty colored bubbles running through the neon tubes. My dad would lift up his little four year-old son and put him on a barstool right between him and mom. Then, like the thoughtful father that he was, he would order me a beer and a polish sausage. I really loved those sausages and you can't eat one without a beer, right? The bartenders at all the places we went knew me by name and I got to do a lot of real neat stuff. I especially liked playing the illegal slot machines and when I would win, I could buy anything I wanted.

What I didn't particularly like was when a fight would break out. If that happened, I would run over to a vacant table in the corner and crawl under it. The other thing I didn't care much for was when my mom and dad would dance and start all that kissing stuff. You see, they never danced with each other. Eventually, I would get tired and crawl up in a booth and go to sleep. The next thing I would remember was being put in the car for the drive home. It was usually a little more difficult to sleep in the car with my parents yelling, cursing and slapping at each other. Finally, we were home and I was in my bed, sometimes in the wee hours of the morning. It wasn't until I was grown that I found out what would happen to my sisters.

They would sit through the movie, then go out front to see if we had come back to pick them up. When we were not there, and we never were, they would go back in and see the movie again. At the end of the second movie, they would call my grandmother to come and bring them to her house. There were times when she would be at a church service very late and not available to come get them. They told me that on more than one occasion, the theater owner was forced to lock up leaving them out on the street alone. They were faced with only one choice and that was to walk the four miles to my grandmother's home. This meant passing through a very bad part of town between 11:00 and 12:00 PM, but after all they were big girls...eight and ten years old at the time.

Things did get a lot better by the time I was ten or so. My parents bought a fishing camp on the river in a cluster of other little camps. Now, we would leave on Friday after my dad got off work and spend the whole weekend camping as a family. Again, I thought this was the kind of camping everyone did. Basically, the routine was the same as before but the location had changed from a bar to the camps. There were parties everywhere and illicit behavior was rampant. This is where I learned about the "birds and bees" by watching the adults as instructors.

I always enjoyed the poker games and my dad was usually kind enough to spot me a couple of dollars to start off with. It seems as though kids are extremely lucky gamblers. I practically always won though it may have had something to do with the fact that I was the only one that was not drunk. Personally, I like to think that I was just good at it. Each weekend seemed to have a story of its own. I remember the weekend when a man who owned a camp close to ours was stabbed in the chest by his girlfriend with a turkey quill. There was another one when I walked in on a couple having sex in my bed in the early afternoon. However, the one that was most difficult for me was the day I came into our camp to see three old guys sitting there watching my mom as she was sleeping off a drunk. She really wasn't that great of a sleeper. The attraction was that she was only wearing her underwear and had no cover over her. What made it worse was that they wouldn't leave when I asked them to. I felt that I had to stay there and guard her until she woke up. Finally, that happened and they left.

Excuse Me … How do I get out of Here?

I was able to talk my dad into buying a little boat with an outboard motor and I would use that to escape in. I would ride for hours up the river and into the small channels. I learned my way around that swamp like it was my neighborhood back home. I became good at fishing, hunting and exploring. There were two men who were avid sportsmen and for some reason they seemed to take a liking to me and taught me many things about the outdoors. My dad never enjoyed any of these activities and preferred to hang around the camp and drink. Thanks to these men, I found some enjoyment and purpose from what could have been a terrible waste of precious time.

I remember that I dreaded Sunday afternoons most of all. My parents would have been drinking since Friday evening and by Sunday, they were always extremely wasted. Once when I was twelve or thirteen I was driving my mother home in our car. She was certainly in no condition to drive and was disgustingly obnoxious. The more she would talk, the angrier I would get and the faster I would drive. I glanced down at the speedometer and saw that I was going well over eighty miles-per-hour and coming up on a forty mile-per-hour curve. I began looking to see what I would hit should I just go straight not even trying to make the curve and discovered that it would have been a house. Even at that age, I knew that wasn't an option. To this day I don't know how the car stayed on the road as we went around that curve so fast. It was truly a miracle and my mother hardly noticed.

By this time my sisters were old enough to have a life of their own with no desire to be a part of this madness any more. There were advantages to being the youngest, but the disadvantage was that I was left alone with my parents after my sisters were gone. I remember envying them and thinking that I couldn't wait until I was old enough to get away from my parents. It seemed as though I was always stressed and anxious, never knowing what they would do next. I was always embarrassed to be their son. I could go on and on but I think you get the picture.

Never Again

Even then, one of my greatest fears was that after I went out on my own I would repeat my parents' behavior and inflict this kind of lifestyle and humiliation on my children. I determined that I would not allow that to happen. When I met the woman who was to be my wife and we decided to marry, I used alcohol and enjoyed going to the clubs. This was the man she was marrying and obviously, the one she wanted. No doubt, she probably expected me to be like this all of our lives. But when my daughter was born, I came home the very first night and cleaned out the liqueur cabinet. Putting everything alcoholic in a box, I got it out of my house. I was very serious about the vow I had made not to bring my daughter up in a home with alcohol in it. From that point on, I seldom drank anything. Oh, from time to time my wife or I would buy a few beers and put them in the refrigerator. But soon, we even stopped doing that.

It was here that one of the problems in my marriage began to surface. You see, my wife had married a man who was content to take her out to the clubs. She enjoyed the music, the dancing and the lifestyle that went with it. It was new and interesting to her. But I had been raised in that environment. I had been there and done that from age four and up. I had witnessed first hand the destruction that comes from that kind of life. I remembered, as I always will, the hurt that is inflicted on children when behavior of this sort infiltrates a family. Neither of my parents saw the need to protect my sisters or me from this. Neither seemed to care what we thought of them, otherwise they may have not behaved so badly. I vowed that I would not allow my daughter to be exposed to what we had experienced.

What I did not realize then was that when I stopped

going with my wife to clubs and began to devote myself totally to my family, in a way it was as if I was going back on an unspoken agreement in my marriage. Since I did these things when my wife married me, she must have assumed that I always would. Now that I wouldn't, she had no one to do them with. This would prove to be the time when our marriage began to die. It would take many years, but it was truly on irreversible path.

I was determined that I would not turn into someone like my dad. I felt that if I did not stop this behavior right now, it might go on for generations to come and I promised that the cycle would be broken and with me. I reasoned that although we might not be a textbook family, we would not be a family like the one I had grown up in. I feel that we can all choose which rut we are in, or even better, we can climb out and take the high ground. I have never liked ruts. There's an old saying that *a rut is just a grave with both ends kicked out of it.* I believe that people who choose to live a destructive life are in something very much like a grave and have little concept of what real living is all about. Life is much too precious to live the way I had seen my parents live.

As damaging as the drinking, fighting and parties were on our childhood, there was one other area that had even more negative impact on me personally. I hated it when my parents fought. Even now, almost fifty years later, I can still recall several times when there were violent fights in our home. Once when I was four or five, I was awakened late at night by yelling and screaming. I tiptoed to the kitchen door, and peeped in. I can still see my dad holding my mother's head down on the kitchen table poking her face with a butcher knife. Although these incidents had a traumatic affect on my sisters and me, it still wasn't as bad as what I would eventually experience.

One night my parents had a party at our house with ten or twelve people all drinking heavily. This was not unusual since practically every weekend one of these parties was held at our house or at the home of one of my parents' friends. As the night would wear on, there would be those in different stages of inebriation with some eventually passing out. This particular night I had been playing with one of the couples' kids. It was very late; I was tired and sleepy and decided to go to my room and to bed. I opened the door and there was my mother and an old friend of our family in my bed. She raised up and yelled at me to get out! My dad was one of those who had long since passed out. Even as an eight or nine-year-old, I was devastated and my little heart seemed to split in two.

One day a short time later, I was outside playing. My dad had a shop in our back yard with a phone in it and I wandered in there and decided to call a friend. When I picked up the phone, I heard him talking to a woman. The shop phone was just an extension of the phone in our house. It was a very graphic conversation and they were making arrangements to meet again. I gently put the phone down and sat on the floor and began to cry. I cried so loudly that eventually he heard me and came out there to see what was wrong. I said that I had fallen and hurt myself. Up until that time, even with his other bad behavior, I still respected and admired his as my dad. From that instant, that respect diminished greatly. It was about thirty years later when I told him about what I had heard. He didn't deny it but said that he didn't remember it happening.

A Bad Dream Comes True

Eventually, my parents' conduct would cause them to face the inevitable. When I was seventeen, I had gone out with the guys one Friday night. We had been riding around and lost track of time. When they put me out at my house, I noticed that all the lights were still on. I assumed that I was in trouble for staying out too late. When I walked into the living room I knew instantly that there was something very seriously wrong. My mom and dad were sitting at a table talking very calmly ... and both sober. They smiled at me and told me to come and sit down. I remember asking myself what could possibly be so important that my dad would be coherent at this late hour. Well, it seems that the contest for who would catch whom first was over and the results were in.

My mother had decided several months earlier to attend a cosmetology school in a nearby city. She had met a serviceman in a nightclub where she would go after she got out of class. She didn't worry much about my dad catching her because of his drinking habits. He was normally out like a light by at least 9:00 PM. What she didn't count on was that his girlfriend was very smart and encouraged him to not drink that night, but rather wait up for her when she came in. My mother and her boyfriend were so sure of themselves that he brought her home that night and drove right up to the front door. My dad came out and chased him but he got away. They went in and decided that a divorce was in order ... which is where I came in.

I was devastated when they told me they would be divorcing. My home was not perfect, certainly not even close. But it was the only one I had known and I didn't want it to break up. I felt sure that if I pleaded enough, I could persuade them to stay together. I always felt loved by both of them even though their behavior didn't always show it. Children are forgiving and I had mentally forgiven them hundreds of times. I knew their shortcomings, but always hoped that they would change and become the kind of parents that some of my friends had. I tried very hard for a couple of days to get them to reconcile. But then I came home from school to find that my mother had moved out. I can't describe the feeling that I had that day. They had argued and fought all of my life, but neither had ever left our home. Not only had she abandoned me, but I realized with her out of our house, the chances of them reconciling was very small. I ran full speed the two miles to the small apartment she had rented and pleaded with her to come back. Their minds were made up and nothing I could say would change that.

For a couple of days, I just kind of wandered around bewildered, thinking until finally I made a decision. I would take control of my own life once and for all. I had been living a life of hope...hoping that they would change; hoping that they would get back together again...when in reality, it had been hopeless. It was then that I decided to move out myself. I would not take sides; I would not choose one over the other. I knew for a fact that they were both guilty of infidelity and I felt that it would not be right for me to take sides. I looked around for a place where I could find stability and had to look no further than my grandparents. I began staying with them and occasionally I would go back and forth between my sisters. I would ultimately finish school moving from house to house while my parents went on with their own lives. Each had chosen a new mate, and it seemed to me that they had chosen them over their son. I truly felt that they both had orphaned me. I began developing some very strong views on the subject of infidelity even at this early age.

Choices

When a parent "falls in love" with someone other than his or her spouse and allows this often temporary emotion to break up their home, a decision has been made the implications of which they would really rather not consider. In doing so, that person is saying:

"I choose to break a vow that I made before God
when I married my spouse.

I choose to bring great pain and anguish upon
this same spouse.

I choose to take my child away from the other
parent for 303 days a year, or,

I may also choose to be away from my child for

*303 days a year, depending on who gets
custody.*

*I choose to put in jeopardy everything my spouse
and I have built or accumulated together.*

*I choose to kill a dream that not only my spouse
and I had but also the dream of my child.*

*I choose to bring shame on myself, my spouse,
my children, and all my family.*

*I choose to bring shame (if I profess to be a
Christian) on the church and the name of
Jesus Christ.*

*I choose to deprive my child of enjoying
Christmas and all other holidays in the
company of both parents.*

*I choose to risk bringing a stranger (my lover)
into my child's life only hoping that there
are no serious consequences.*

*I choose to take the chance of being alone possi-
bly for the rest of my life, if this new relationship doesn't work out.*

*I choose to allow my child's life to be disrupted
week after week by the process of visitation.*

*I choose to cause my child to cry himself to sleep
for countless nights.*

*I choose to put myself in the position of possibly
having to work outside the home for the
rest of my life.*

*In that case, I choose to put my child in a day-
care institution delegating his or her
upbringing to non-relatives and strangers.*

*I choose to risk that my child will completely
lose contact with his other parent.*

*I choose to put at risk my child's emotional sta-
bility that could change the course of his
life forever.*

*I choose to cause God to grieve over the break-
up of my family.*

*I choose to bring guilt upon myself for causing
     so many so much pain.*
*I choose to inflict all these things and more on
     the spouse, my children, and the children
     of my lover.*
*I choose to do all of these things and many oth-
     ers as well so that I can fulfill my own self-
     ish desires.*

Of course, this is not the way that the spouse who is breaking up the marriage would express it. But in actual fact, this is what it amounts to.

You may say, "But you don't know what it's like. You don't understand how deeply I desire this and how much I need to do what I am doing."

You're right... I don't. All I know is what it's like to be a child of divorce and I also know what it is like to be a spouse who is rejected and no longer wanted. I know what it is to have a broken heart over a broken home. I know how it feels to grieve over a wonderful child who will never have the life that God intended for her.... one with a mother and a father who love each other, are happy with each other, and committed to each other and their family. No, I don't know what it is like to want passion with someone new that I hardly know more than I want what is best for my family. I don't want to know what that is like and I hope I never will.

It seems that far too many parents are making the choices listed above regardless of the consequences. I determined that, should I have a child, she would never have to experience a childhood like mine. She would have a father who not only loved her...I know that both my parents loved their kids...but one who was "involved" in her life. As a young boy, I was never proud of my dad. I always looked at some of the other kids' dads and wished I had been born to one of them. I knew that I wanted to be a father whose kid could be proud of him.

One More Choice

I later realized that many children come from dysfunctional homes and make a choice not to allow that to adversely affect their lives. I also understand that some truly are affected by it and do not have the power to overcome its impact on their life. One thing that I do know for sure is that there were several times when I made a decision not to allow negative circumstances to ruin my life. When I thought about it and I made these decisions consciously, the result was usually positive.

I am reminded of someone quite remarkable whom we will call Trish. She was born in a northern city to a family with comfortable means, but who were certainly not wealthy. Her mother was a Christian lady who did the best she could to raise Trish and her three brothers in a good and moral way. Trish's father, however, was not like her mother. He was a common working man with several destructive habits. One such habit was that he liked going out making his round of the bars. One night when he had been drinking far too much, he came home and crossed the unthinkable line that no father should ever cross. He came in to Trish's room when she was about 11 and touched her in a sexual way. She had always idolized her dad and didn't know how to respond to this new relationship that he was proposing. He just reassured her that she was still his little girl and that he loved her so much that they needed more than what most fathers and daughters had.

Unfortunately, it progressed to the point that it was more like a marriage than a father-child relationship. As she got older, he would even take her with him to his favorite bars not allowing any other man to get close to her. This incestuous behavior went on until she was about 14 and she was finally courageous enough to put a stop to it. At 15 she ran away from home to another state and moved in with a young man whom she eventually married.

In getting to know Trish and talking with her, I soon realized that she was incredibly strong. Did she have hurts? Of course and they were always brought to mind whenever she thought of her father. But I was most impressed with her strength and tenacity. At some point, she had made a decision that she would not allow what this man had done to her to ruin her life. She would decide for herself what she wanted and go after it... relentlessly. At this writing, she is 25, still married to the young husband of her youth, has a beautiful one year old baby boy, owns her own home and is a stay at home mom. Several years ago, she took her GED and has recently enrolled in college. Pretty successful I would say, and all because she decided to live in the present and put the past behind her.

As for my parents, I have seen first hand two people making all of the wrong choices and having to live through the results. I have thought about it many times but have been unable to come up with even one positive thing they left to their children. After over forty years of parenting, there should have been many good things that they did that their children could remember happily and tell others about. Now that I think about it, I guess I could say that my dad was kind to me and my mother loved me a lot. But they had all those years to teach me things that would make me a better person. I had to learn those things from others. Of course, one way of thinking of it would be to say that they did teach me in their own way. By example, they taught me how not to live my life and the things to stay far away from. No one I know will recommend this method of instruction.

How Will We be Remembered?

Is that the legacy that you want to leave your child? Someday after you are gone, your child will be telling someone about the impact that you had on him. I have heard far too many adults talk about their lack of love and affection in their home as they were growing up.

Many men in particular have never heard their dad tell them that he loved them. What makes that such a hard thing for men to do? I hope that your child is hearing that he is loved and that he is very special to you.

There is sort of a happy ending to the saga of my parents. Eventually, they both managed to clean up their act. My mother remarried twice and came to Christ some fifteen or so years before she died. My dad was divorced from his second wife and lived in a small house we built for him next door to mine until his death at age 63 of a heart attack. We were business partners until he retired and had become best friends in those later years. Both in their own way, shared with me the regrets that haunted them concerning the way they had chosen to live and treat their kids. My mom in particular carried her shame and remorse with her to her death. It was comforting to know that a time came when they both wished that their conduct had been different. It's sad to say, by that time the damage had been done. Precious years had been wasted and what is more important, three children's lives had been adversely affected by their actions. They themselves had lived very unhappy lives and only in their last years did they experience even a small amount of happiness and fulfillment.

By the way, earlier, I said that my parents had not seen the need to protect us from the lifestyle they had chosen to live. However, there were two people who had tried...two people whom God had placed in our lives to be used by him to care for us and set an example. They made a valiant attempt to be to us what our parents never were and they never gave up. These were two people I will never forget and I still miss them terribly even today. When I think of having parents in the sense of who did the job rather than who held the titles, I think of them. In the following chapter, I would like to make an attempt to convey something of who they were and what they meant to me. In doing this, I also hope to show the value and importance of a role model in the life of a child.

7

Is There a Role Model in the House?

A Pattern to Live By

Picture if you will, waking in the middle of the night to discover that there is a power outage. You need to check on some things, but it is very dark. "Where's my flashlight?" you think. Then, you catch yourself saying, "If only I had a flashlight, I could use it to find my flashlight", at least that's the way I think at 3:00 AM. I realize this may sound a little ridiculous, but bear with me. It should be apparent from what was said in the previous chapter that my parents did not set a good example for me. Somehow, I knew that I needed someone to pattern my life after, but that person did not share the same address as me. If my parents had made even a little effort to guide me in the right direction, they would have been like that temporary flashlight I needed to locate my real one. Fortunately, my real one was so bright that I had no problem finding it. It was my grandparents and they would outshine all others.

My mom's parents always lived very close by our home when I was growing up. I was at their house almost as much as I was at my own home. My grandmother had been 14 and my grandfather 22 when they met and were married. These were two young people of another era who made a lifelong commitment to each other and always honored it. I'm not sure how it happened, but all their grandchildren called them "Mama and Daddy." I never thought much about it at the time. It was like God knew from the beginning that my parents would not be adequate and gave me these wonderful grandparents as a backup.

Mama

My grandmother was a devout Christian lady who loved God as much as anyone I have ever known. She would sit in her rocking chair and pray for an hour at a time. Now when she prayed, it wasn't in quiet little sentences with tender heartfelt requests. She would bellow out her prayers, crying and wailing so loud that the neighbors far away could hear. It was because of this that they all seemed to know our family business. Mama would do this at least twice and sometimes three times a day, seven days a week for as long as I can remember. She would pray for every member of her family, followed by praying for her church family until everyone was covered in a blanket of prayer. She loved her church and it was most important to her second only to her family. She never had a piano lesson in her whole life, but she was the church pianist for forty years. If I were staying with her on a church night, she would dress me up and drag me by my ear with her. I never liked going to her church because as a very small child, I was frightened by their demonstrative worship.

My grandmother often talked to me about the Lord. She would read from the Bible and explain in her own way what she read. There were also many Bible stories that she would tell me as I sat on her lap. I also remember one non-Bible story in particular that she loved. She told me the story so many times that I had it memorized. She had been a little girl when the Titanic went down, but since that was the biggest story of its time, she had heard it repeated over and over. She would emphasize that the people on board had thought that the ship was unsinkable and that they were doing a lot of sinful things on board like "drinking, dancing and who knows what else," she would say. Then she would get to the part where the ship was going down and the band was playing *"Nearer My God To Thee."* Every time she would say, "See son, it took the ship sinking to bring that bunch to the Lord." Her point was that I, even as a little boy, needed to surrender my life to God even then. She was much more than a grandmother to me. She was a wonderful and much needed mother.

Daddy

Second only to her God, the man she had married when she was so very young was most important to her. My grandfather was the most remarkably unique man I have ever known. My feelings about him even today are so strong that I get emotional when I think of him. No one else has ever had the impact on my life that he has, and no one else ever will. I will try to describe him, but I doubt that anyone who didn't know him could ever completely understand what was so great about him.

First, he was a working man. It was from him that I learned about the honor that comes from hard work. He owned a small nursery where he grew mostly azaleas and camellias. They were his passion and he seemed to be happiest when he was in his greenhouse or hoeing the rows of plants in the field. I remember being in the kitchen one day and I saw him through the window coming toward the house. As he entered the kitchen where everyone else was, he said, "Look at this! Just look at it!" He was holding in his hand a variegated (Multi-colored) camellia bloom. His eyes sparkled as he held it up in front of him. "Have you ever seen anything like this in all your life?" I remember looking up at it and thinking, "What's the big deal? I've seen lots of those before." Well, the big deal was that my grandfather was the expert and had a very discriminating eye. He was in awe of the perfect beauty of this flower. It was special to him since he had grown the plant that produced it from a cutting—literally a twig. Now, it's purpose for existence had been fulfilled. It had produced a miracle in his eyes and he was so happy about it.

I have thought a lot about that experience over the years. My grandfather was the proud father of a beautiful, perfect flower. He had nurtured it for months and it was finally mature. This is how every parent should feel when they see their children grow and mature into what is their true purpose in life. It is for this special reason they were created and their real beauty is finally revealed. In the same sense, imagine our Heavenly Father holding his beautiful flower in his hand. This flower is your life. Is he as pleased and proud as my grandfather was? It could be that right now, you might not want him to examine your life very closely. There may be far too many flaws that you would rather that He didn't see. Truthfully, he has already seen them. Now he is waiting for you to allow him to make you beautiful again. He can do that you know—if you will let him.

God … Is That You?

As a small boy, when I tried to visualize what God looked like, I saw him as my grandfather. As I grew older I came to understand that God probably didn't wear a straw hat, khaki work pants, and old beat up work boots. For the most part, my grandfather ran a one-man operation. When he needed help, sometimes he would ask me to go and work with him. At times I would help him in the field weeding or hoeing the camellia plants. At other times I might be digging new potatoes, harvesting corn, or climbing up and shaking pecan trees for those who would be picking up the nuts for pennies a pound. But my most dreaded job was going out with him to other homes in town to spray camellias and azaleas for insects. He used a large contraption mounted on a wheelbarrow-type apparatus consisting of a drum containing the chemicals mixed with water. It had a long handle that operated the pump, which transferred the chemicals to a hose with a spray nozzle on the end. My job was to move the heavy apparatus as needed to keep up with him and at the same time use the hand pump to keep up the pressure for spraying. I was always afraid the pressure would get low and he would have to scold me. I was as determined as any young boy could be to keep him supplied with sufficient pressure, which put me under even greater pressure.

Whatever we were doing, I would work very hard and at the end of the day he would give me a dollar... sometimes two. I was happy about the money, but mostly my hard work was for one reason and one only: to please him. He was my hero. I had placed him on a pedestal and all my life I watched to see if he could stay there.

Here was a true paradox. He was the strongest man I have ever known, yet so tender that his eyes teared up when he looked at God's creation. He was one whom we all feared; yet we depended on him for our own protection. Honesty was not just his best policy; it was his only policy. Yet no one I have ever known had a quicker and more violent temper. He was morally impeccable except for the fact that he could let go of curse words using the Lord's name in vain and go on and on until he would become pale and weak. He was patient with the babies in our family, but exercised little or no patience with the tools of his trade, politicians or bad guys on television.

Speaking of which, he also had a unique sense of humor. I used to sit for long periods of time and watch him as he watched TV. He would carry on conversations with the characters yelling at them when they deserved it. One of his favorites was Perry Mason. I have heard him on countless occasions yell at and curse the District Attorney. Then, when Perry would win an argument in court, he would laugh loud enough that everyone in the house could hear him.

Once I was working in the field with him when his tractor stalled. It had a hand crank on the front so he got off and proceeded to turn it over and over. The engine would not start, and eventually, he became exhausted and collapsed to his knees still cursing and turning the crank—but the tractor never responded. He calmly got up and walked the three hundred yards to the barn. As he was coming back I saw a steel axle in his hand. He walked up to the tractor and began hitting it over and over again with the axle. It made huge dents in the metal, but he kept hitting it. Once again, he got weak and went to his knees while cursing. Then it was over. He did a little adjusting to the carburetor and the tractor cranked. This was just the way Daddy did things. As upsetting as these tirades were to the family, they had no effect on the respect we gave him. He had obtained that respect the old fashioned way... he had earned it.

Just the Way They Were

I didn't just decide one day that these two people would be my role models. They took the job while overwhelming any other competition that may have been around. And yet I don't think that they were consciously competing for the position. This was just who they were...it was the way they lived their lives. They would have been this way if no children or grandchildren had existed. No one would ever steal my grandmother's faith and my grandfather would live 73 years as a man of unchallenged integrity.

In addition to his temper, I can tell you with great certainty that my grandfather had another great fault as well. He had been born in Savannah, Georgia in 1898... in the "Old South." When he was growing up, Black people had no rights and were routinely treated as sub-human. He later moved to South Mississippi and married my grandmother settling down in her hometown a few years prior to 1920. The prejudice that he exhibited had been handed down to him by his father. He was intolerant of any form of disrespect from those of the Black race and was very out-spoken about his views. Everyone in town knew where he stood on this issue. His reputation was such that I can remember seeing Black men walking down the road and as they approached his property, they would cross over to the other side. None wanted a confrontation with "Mr. Tom.".

At about 72, he became very ill and his health began to deteriorate rapidly. This was very difficult for all of us since he had always been so strong. Now, he was dependent upon everyone around him and he obviously didn't like that at all. He was gruff, angry and very short with everyone. He was a rather well-built and muscular man and far too heavy for my grandmother and aunt to lift. It became necessary to hire someone to help with him. A Black man was given the job and in a gentle and respectful way, he began winning my grandfather's confidence.

When I think back, it seems amazing to me that he had lived his whole life without becoming a Christian. Oh, he attended church with my grandmother frequently, sitting on the back row and listening intently to every word that the preacher spoke. He never had anything bad to say about her faith, but also never chose to join her in it. One day while bedridden, he called for her pastor to come see him. That was the day that he accepted Christ and was born again. Instantly, we saw a change in his temperament, his demeanor, and the way he responded to everyone around him. It was obvious that he wasn't the same. It was also about this time that his prejudice began to disappear. He would laugh and talk with the Black man hired to take care of him and ironically, they became great friends. This was a milestone for my grandfather to give up seventy plus years of radical hatred for those of the Black race, but with the love of Christ in him, there was no room for hating anyone.

His Last Words

A few months later his condition deteriorated to the point that he was moved to the hospital. I was called to come and was told that he probably would not live but a few days. One night I was sitting outside his hospital room when someone came and said to me, "Daddy wants to see you." I went in and walked over to his bedside. My grandmother said, "Tom, Wayne is here." He mumbled something that I couldn't understand. I moved closer as he repeated what he had said to me but still couldn't understand since he was so weak and very close to death. I finally leaned over and put my ear directly over his mouth saying, "What do you want to tell me Daddy?" Once more he spoke and this time I understood what it was that he wanted so badly to tell me before he died. "Son," he said, "you are too good of a boy to be lost." I was already hurting just seeing him this way and knowing that the end was so near. He was my idol, my role model, my hero, my Daddy. I felt as though my heart would explode. Somehow, I managed to maintain my composure as I left the room. He had lived his whole life with the utmost honesty and integrity, but had never tried to win anyone to the Lord. He would at least try to influence me, his grandson before he left this world.

It was only a short time later when someone came out and told me to come back into his room. As I walked in, everyone had that look on their faces; the look that said, "This is it." I stood there for what seemed to be a very long time looking at his face. His eyes were closed but he would flinch from time to time. Memories flooded my mind and I thought of my life with this wonderful person. His nickname for me was "Man." When I was just a little thing, he would call to me, "Man, come go with me." I would follow this towering figure outside as he walked toward the field. As he would work, he might sing one of the old songs of his youth, or ask me questions just to see what I would say. Then, when he finished, he would say,

"Man, I'll race you to the store for a cold drink." Off we would go full speed with him out ahead. The store was right across the road from his house. About twenty feet or so from the door, he would start slowing down allowing me to pass him. "Oh! You beat me again," he would say as he laughed. Then we would enjoy one of the coldest soft drinks on the planet. He had been a wonderful grandfather to me. But more than that, he had been an extraordinary father.

It was while standing there looking down at him and thinking of all of those great times we had together, that I saw him do something that was so familiar. Anytime that he was straining to pick up a heavy object or do something very hard, his whole face would grimace. Watching as he did this, I saw him take his last breath, and his face relaxed. It was over. He had raised his children and his grandchildren and had witnessed to me and now he could die. Those last words that he had whispered in my ear would remain with me for the rest of my life. They would be used over and over to draw me to Christ until I finally gave in. We all should want to leave a worthwhile legacy after we are gone. My grandfather left one that would never die. I would see to that.

The Legacy Must Live On

My grandmother outlived him by almost twenty years but eventually went to join both of the loves of her life, Tom and Jesus, in heaven. They were far from wealthy, but I have a storehouse full of treasures that they left to me, memories too precious to place a price on them. There are times even now when matters of faith will cause me to question my motives and I immediately ask myself what Mama's reaction would be. Then, when I am forced to make a decision relating to honesty and what is right, I always ask, "What would Daddy do?" I know that his response to any situation concerning honesty and ethics would be the right one. I had been truly blessed to have these wonderful people in my life. I pity those who have no one to exercise a positive influence on them, no one to look up to.

Even before I married, I remember thinking that when it came time for me to be a father, I would step up to the plate and be the role model in my child's life. She would not have to leap over a generation to find someone to pattern her life after. I took this very seriously because when I was a child myself, it was serious to me. I believe that children in many families are starving for an adult to be the one they can look up to. They feel the need to learn life habits and they will learn them from someone—if not from their parents, then from someone else. How tragic it is if neither their parents nor anyone else around them is a person of integrity worthy to offer them an example to follow. It is equally sad when they have a spiritual void in their life that a parent is not helping them to fill.

As a child and an adolescent, I always feared letting my grandparents down. Don't get me wrong. I did a lot of things that I am not proud of, but I was very careful to make sure that they didn't find out about those things. I would have been crushed to see a look of disappointment on my grandfather's face and to know that I was the one that had failed him. And, I know that if my grandmother had known of some of the things I did, her heart would have been broken. To see them disappointed in me would have broken my heart as well. Because I did not disappoint them, they thought I was special and seemed to love me in a very special way. Now as I think about it, they probably loved me so much because they knew how much I wanted them to be proud of me. I got special treatment from them and I sensed it even then. They showed that they were proud of me and I just couldn't allow myself to disappoint them.

This is the way I always wanted my daughter to feel about me. I knew first hand that if she cared that much about what I thought about her, it would mean that she loved and respected me as much as I had my grandparents. At the same time, I knew that I had an obligation to be the kind of parent that she could be proud of...so much so that she would never be ashamed to say that I was her dad. And Casey will know that if her dad leaves her nothing else, he will leave memories of a father who cared deeply for her and one who also didn't want to disappoint her.

8

Where is the Lamb?

Hold Nothing Back

What would you be willing to do for God? The standard answer given by many Christians might be..."anything." Really? What if God asked you to quit your job, sell all of your belongings and move? Would you do it? Maybe you would. What would you **NOT** do for God? Would you give up your only child, sacrificing him—losing him forever? You may say, "**God would never ask me to do that.**" You think not?

Abraham had a son named Isaac. I feel that I can imagine how very much he loved him. God had promised him a child but so many years had gone by and none was born. Abraham and Sarah grew old and were far past the time in life when people normally have children. Then an amazing miracle happened! Sarah bore Abraham a son! God had promised Abraham that this would happen and Isaac was truly a miracle child, a gift from God. How Sarah and Abraham must have rejoiced to see the blessed child grow into young manhood! Then one day God spoke these terrible words to Abraham: *"Take your son, your only son, Isaac, whom you love, and go to the region of Moriah. Sacrifice him there as a burnt offering on one of the mountains I will tell you about."*

The next morning Abraham took his son Isaac and two servants and departed toward the mountain that God had indicated. They took the wood for the fire and a knife. When they were near to the mountain, Abraham left the two servants to wait for them and taking Isaac, continued on to the appointed place. On the way, Isaac said to his father, *"The fire and the wood are here, but where is the lamb for the burnt offering?"* Abraham said to his son, *"God Himself will provide the lamb for the burnt offering, my son."* Centuries later, Christians would understand the two-fold meaning of Abraham's answer.

First, in this statement, he revealed his enormous faith that God would somehow spare his son, even if it took raising him from the dead. Then, these prophetic words also predicted that the only Son of God, the Lamb of Glory, Jesus Christ, would be made a sacrifice for the sins of the world. Obediently, Abraham bound his son, placed him on the altar and upon the wood for the fire. Then he reached out his hand and took the knife to kill his son. But God stopped him saying, *"Do not lay a hand on the boy. Now I know that you fear God, because you have not withheld from me your son, your only son."*

Great philosophers and theologians have discussed for centuries the rich array of meanings in this ancient story. For Jews, it embodied a sense of God's providing for, and leading, the people he had made the object of his divine covenant. For Christians it symbolized God's provident care for his people and his demand that they obey him and put him first in their lives. It also involves the assurance that when we surrender to God all that we have, all that is most precious to us, then God will not deprive us of our heart's desire, but will fill our lives with everything that we really need.

Fine for Abraham, but What About Me?

It may be that Abraham understood God to be saying that he must not love anything, even his only son, more than he loved God. But what was the message that I could understand God to be trying to communicate to me through this great story from antiquity? As I saw it, Casey was my daughter, my only daughter. She was my miracle and as precious to me as Isaac was to Abraham. When

God told Abraham to sacrifice Isaac, it was like he was revoking custody and taking him back to live with him. God didn't want anything or anyone between Abraham and himself. God never wants to take second place and once he saw that he was first with Abraham, it was not necessary for Isaac to be sacrificed. It was here that he gave Isaac to Abraham for the second time.

At a point in my life when I felt most abandoned by my daughter, I was earnestly seeking answers. I felt that my role in her life as father was not only in jeopardy, but was diminishing at a fast rate. In prayer one evening, God impressed several things upon me. I recognized that I was probably never going to be able to keep the vow to be there and care for my daughter on a daily basis. She was to live out her childhood with her mother as her custodial parent and I would see her only sporadically. It was then that I finally decided to give her up. No, I would never stop trying to be with her and certainly wasn't relinquishing my fatherly duties. But here, in my mind, I placed her on the altar and gave her to God trusting that he would do the same thing for me that he had done for Abraham. Someday I just knew that he would give her back to me and our relationship would be blessed by what had happened.

Then, mentally, I released my daughter from whatever obligation that I had imposed upon her to spend time with me. When she would come to see me, I was thrilled. When she chose to stay away, I filled my time with other things so that I wouldn't dwell on what seemed at the time to be rejection.

Was I still hurt and sad? Of course. I would spend hours thinking of how things should have been. I had always wanted to be there when she had her first date. I wanted to look that young man in the eyes and let him know that there was a "dad in the house." I wanted to make sure that he knew that there were consequences for his behavior should he be dumb enough to be anything other than a perfect gentleman. I wanted to be around when she had a problem that only a dad could deal with. But since I could not be with her on a daily basis, I would not be able to help her when such a problem occurred. In fact, many times the problem would have been resolved before I ever knew about it. I wanted to be there to tuck her in…even at sixteen, and tell her I love her and that Jesus loves her. I missed being with her when she was heartbroken over a boy who didn't recognize her for what she was …the most special young lady ever. I missed waking her in the morning and spending time alone with her before she would go off to school.

Most of all, I just missed watching her. I have always loved to watch her do things … anything. She had the most wonderful walk and I lived to just sit and watch her walk around the house. I also loved to watch her laugh and act silly. She was always so full of life that it filled me to the brim just being around her. I remember watching her sleep while marveling at those perfect little lips as she sucked on her thumb. She was my greatest joy and I just wanted to watch her.

I remember thinking how blessed my ex-wife was to be able to live with our daughter. Then it occurred to me that maybe she needed her more than I did, though it was hard for me to imagine how. If being wanted is good for a child, and I know that it is, our little girl would surely turn out OK. There was never enough of her to go around. I vowed to pray for her every day and ask God to do for her what I could not; protect and nurture her every day of her life. I also began praying for the young man whom she would someday marry. Of course, at this time I had no idea who that would be. I did know that he would have to be very special and I couldn't imagine anyone being worthy to be the husband of my little girl.

I remember one night after she was in her teens I had taken her out to dinner and I was driving very slowly toward her home. She made some remark and I recognized it as a teaching moment. I began making a lesson out of the situation and she said, "Daddy, you are always lecturing me." I told her that if we lived together, these lessons could be taught partly by example. Then I wouldn't feel the need to present them as lectures. But since I saw her so seldom, I felt that I had to compress a lot of counseling into a very short time span. After that, though, I tried to be more subtle, but nevertheless, there was so much I wanted to teach her and continued to do so whenever the opportunity would present itself. One of the most important things I wanted her to learn most was responsibility.

She Begins to Blossom

Soon I began seeing the fruits of my labor and I was not just proud—I was amazed. She decided that she wanted to work and earn some of her own money. So after looking around for a while, she got a job in a yogurt shop. She handled herself well and was very dependable. From there, she went on to a couple of other part time jobs before she settled down at the YMCA. It was here that she showed me that she had been listening all those years as I sought to teach her to be responsible and trustworthy. She was an exceptional employee and was soon promoted to site director. She worked at the Y through high school and two years of college.

Because of her level of maturity and responsibility, I decided that I would buy her a car when she was a sophomore in high school. It would enable her to go to school all day and then on to work until 6:00 PM. She took all of the training programs that the Y offered and sometimes did this on her own time. She worked well with the children at her after school camp and was hired to work summer camp when the school year ended.

From the time she was a junior in high school, I began to see a transition in her attitude toward me. She became much more sensitive to my feelings and became increasingly more receptive to spending time with me. This thrilled me and I was thankful for every hour we had together. Over the next few years we would do some things together that weren't very common for a father and daughter. I won a drawing at a lumber store and the prize was a weekend in New Orleans. Included were two nights accommodations in a very nice hotel in the French Quarter. Also included was dinner for two at a great restaurant along with tickets to a Saints football game. We walked together for miles in the city, holding hands and talking about my life, her life, my future, her future and who knows what else. We enjoyed ourselves immensely and I will always look back on that weekend with great fondness.

It was during times like these that we really got to know each other as fellow human beings, not just father and daughter. I learned a lot about her and she probably discovered things about me that she didn't know. Dads, if you don't spend this kind of time with your child, you should. Please appreciate and savor every moment that you have with them. Be innovative as you do things with them that will make a memory that will last forever. Think about the memories you have as a child with your parents. Are they pleasant? If so, all the more reason to give your children the wonderful gift of pleasant memories with a parent who will love them and sacrifice time for them. Your private memories may mean little to your child. Her private memories may mean little to you, but the memories you make together mean everything to both of you.

Meanwhile, I had become acquainted with a young man named Jacob who worked at a lumberyard where I did quite a bit of business. In talking with him, I sensed a kind spirit with humility and honesty all rolled up into one. He and I would talk briefly while he helped me load my truck and I grew to like him. One evening my daughter and I were out having dinner together and she told me that she was seeing someone that I knew. I was pleasantly surprised to find out that it was Jacob. I asked her the usual fatherly questions about him and finally came to the one about his faith. She told me that he was a Christian but did not attend church.

Time passed and they were seeing a lot of each other. Months later she told me that they were talking about marriage. I said that sounded fine but that Jacob needed to talk to me about it too. She said that he wasn't going to like that very much but she would tell him. One day we were having lunch together and she mentioned that she might be getting engaged soon. I asked her again if she really thought he was a Christian. I could tell by her answer that down deep she knew that he wasn't. As we were eating, I told her that I would do almost anything for her. Yet as deeply as I loved her, there was something I could never do. I couldn't walk her down the aisle and give her away to someone who was not a Christian. She never looked up, but as she ate, tears began to roll down her cheeks. A part of me wanted to say, "Never mind what I just said Sweetheart, I will do it." Yet I knew that she was too precious to me and the Lord for it to be any other way.

Another Prayer is Answered

Months passed and Christmas was nearing. Jacob was planning to give her an engagement ring for her gift but she reminded him that he still needed to talk to me. I was beginning to wonder if it would ever happen when finally, one Saturday he called to see if I would be at home. He brought his new rifle, I got mine and off we went for a walk out to the creek to shoot our guns. Jacob is quite a sportsman. He loves hunting and fishing and anything pertaining to either. I had spent my teen years learning nearly everything there was to know about hunting and fishing so I understood his love for these things and it gave us an important interest in common. Yet we both knew where our most important common interest lie.

After several hours of relative small talk, it seemed that we were no nearer to the reason that he had come than when he had first arrived. I decided I'd better see if I could help a little. "Casey tells me that you two are thinking about getting married," I said. Slowly he responded, "Yes, well, I guess that depends on you." Wow! What an answer! This was probably the perfect answer for a young man hoping to win his future father-in-law's approval. I remember thinking "Yes! He's definitely worth the effort." Well, you and I both know that they probably would have married regardless of what I thought, but I realized that this was one of the most courteous things anyone has ever said to me.

I didn't waste any time. "Jake, are you a Christian?" He thought a minute and said, "I guess so. My mom used to take me to Sunday school when I was little." I had my answer. We don't "guess so" about this issue. I know that Walter Hudson was my dad and I know that Jesus Christ is my Savior. Being a Christian isn't what we are, but rather who we are. Once you have met Jesus, you know it. I believe that the experience of coming to know Christ is an event, not an evolutionary process. We tend to remember the dramatic, the moving, and the emotional experiences of our life. At the moment we recognize Jesus as the Savior and choose to accept his sacrifice for our sins, we should be extremely moved and very emotional. We should never forget this and should always recognize it as the great event of our life.

So I asked Jacob, "But has there ever been a time when you invited Christ into your heart and determined to live for Him?" His response was, "No." His honesty was refreshing and I was relieved for now we had a place to begin. I began telling him what Christianity was all about. I started with the fall of man in the Garden of Eden and twenty minutes later arrived at the cross, explaining why it was necessary for Jesus to die for us there. I explained how I had prayed with Casey when she was about five and she received Christ and had been living for Him ever since. I used an analogy about two dogs in a race. One had all four legs and the other had only three. The leg that was missing on the one dog was the "spiritual leg", literally a relationship with Christ. I told him that Casey had that fourth leg and that it was unnatural to put someone with four legs in a race with another who had one missing.

He had been listening intently and it had become apparent that his interest was genuine. I told him that Casey was the most important person in the world to me and that I wanted only the best for her. I said that I had been watching him for a long time and that with only one exception, I approved of their plans. I asked him if he would like to have all four legs so that he could properly run the race of life with my daughter. He said, "Yes". So late that afternoon out on a creek's sandbar, the Lord gave me the wonderful privilege of leading to Christ the young man whom I had been praying for since Casey was about twelve. I hugged him and told him I loved him and welcomed him to the family. He spent quite a while with me after that before he left for home. It was obvious that he was more relaxed and relieved. I am not sure if it was because he had just become a Christian or that he had finally had the little talk with me he had been dreading so long. Either way, we were both very happy people.

As he left, I went up to my bedroom window and watched his taillights as he drove down my driveway. My thoughts went back to that day in the restaurant when I told my daughter that I could never give her away to someone who wasn't a Christian. I picked up the phone and dialed. "Hello Sweetheart." She responded very nervously, "Hi Daddy, is Jacob still there with you? I have been a nervous wreck waiting to hear from him. What have you two been doing all this time?" I said, "He is just leaving and I have some good news. I can walk you down that aisle now Sweetheart. He just accepted Christ." When I hung up the phone I fell to my knees and thanked God for this answer to my prayer. He is truly faithful.

That was a very good day…for all three of us. I was allowed to keep yet another vow that I had made years before. My daughter would not be marrying a non-believer. She would be starting with a Christian home and have the advantage so many never have. Her life would be different…it would be much better. And Jacob? Well, it was the day that he became a member of the family—the family of God, that is. I felt sure that his life would never be the same.

Finally … A Merry Christmas

Christmas came and she got her engagement ring. I had never seen her happier and because of that, I was also very happy. This time, I just knew that I had the right Christmas present for her. I had put more thought into this one than ever before. I had started in November looking for just the perfect gift. I had no idea what it would be, but I felt that I would know it when I saw it. I looked everywhere at so many different kinds of things, but none seemed to be right for her. Finally, it hit me. Every girl, especially one who is engaged, would love to have a hope chest. I remember thinking, "Wayne Hudson, you truly are a genius. This time you've got it right." I searched everywhere and finally found a beautiful cedar chest with hand carving and purchased it for her.

On Christmas morning she and Jacob came to my house so that we could exchange gifts. I saved her **"big"** gift for last and as she opened it, I couldn't wait for the expression of surprise and happiness to appear on her face. I was so proud of myself. I was such a great shopper after all. But what I saw was that same look that I had seen that Christmas when she was twelve. Oh well, I learn from my mistakes and so I assured her that we would exchange it for the treadmill she had really wanted. Women! Who can figure them out? But she did keep what was in the chest. I had spent most of the week writing something for her to go in her hope chest that she could keep long after I was gone.

* * * * * * * * *

"My Dear Daughter,

Hope is a great thing. It keeps us going when we want to quit. It gives us something to live for when we want to die. It's the thing that gets us out of bed each morning and brings the peace required for us to go to sleep at night. It's the thing that makes us get back up when we are knocked down. Hope motivates us to take that next step and make that next decision. Without hope we have no purpose, no motivation, no goals.

My hope for this time in your life is that you may be the happiest woman on this earth and I hope that happiness endures forever.

I hope that you learn the true secret to happiness. Genuine happiness comes from a close, committed, right relationship with our Lord Jesus Christ and from investing yourself in the lives of others.

I hope that when you think of your Daddy, you think happy thoughts as I do when I think of you.

And finally, I hope you have a daughter as wonderful as mine someday.
I love you,
Daddy 12/24/96"

9

Father of the Bride

Yet Another Loss

I was sitting on a wide body 747 coming home from Europe. It had been an experience I would never forget. Forty-nine other people and I had just spent ten days witnessing, leading people to the Lord, and passing out New Testament Bibles in Moscow and Romania. We estimated that about 5,000 had received Christ and over 68,000 Bibles were distributed. I had experienced something that previously I had only heard about. I looked into the faces of hundreds of people who for over 70 years had been forbidden to worship God. I saw them come up to us on the streets with no hope and walk away as new creations with the hope of Christ in their hearts.

This was a unique time in history. The old Soviet Union had been closed to the Gospel since Lenin took office. That had been a drastic measure for a country that was once devoutly Christian. In 989, Vladimir was baptized and Russia converted to Christianity. In 1550, construction of the Cathedral of St. Basil the Blessed began in Red Square. Until the coming of Communism, Christianity had been the cornerstone of life in Russia.

I found it very interesting that in 1918, separation of church and state began along with the persecution of the Russian Orthodox Church. It was just four years later when the USSR was formed under Lenin. In 1927, Stalin took control and under his godless reign, millions would die as he sought to purge his country. Finally came the new revolution of 1991 and the USSR was dissolved. The following year, religious freedom was renewed. The Orthodox

Church, which had been underground for seventy years, reappeared and reasserted its supremacy.

The notorious Communist dictator, Ceausescu, had ruled Romania until December 1989. A few days before Christmas, in the town of Timasoara, Father Lasso Toques spoke out publicly from the pulpit of his church condemning the actions of Ceausescu. The result would be an all out revolution in Timasoara and Bucharest. In a matter of days it was over, Ceausescu was executed and this country too was open again to the Gospel of Christ.

It was 1992 now and thousands of Christians from all over the world had been allowed to enter Russia and Romania with the message of the Gospel. Millions had received Christ and these countries were now experiencing another type of revolution. The Lord had opened the door to these countries one more time. In doing so, Christians rushed in and these wonderful people responded by the thousands. How long this kind of freedom would be allowed to continue, no one but the Lord knew. I am thankful that he had been gracious enough to allow me to be a small part of this miracle.

Is That Really Me?

My mind was flooded with thoughts and memories of the trip when I looked at one of the plane's TV monitors in front of me and saw something that would make me forget about everything else. It was Steve Martin. I recognized the title caption as one my daughter had told me about. I could almost hear her voice saying, "Dad, there's this movie and you've just got to see it. The father in the movie reminds me so much of you. You just have to go see it." Well, I never got around to it but now, here I was thousands of feet in the air and thousands of miles from home about to watch the movie she wanted me to see. It was *"FATHER OF THE BRIDE."*

In the first place, I don't think that I look anything like Steve Martin and I know that I'm not as funny as he is. So let's see what she's talking about. I watched and began to understand what she had meant. There were several times that I caught tears welling up as I saw Martin's love for his little girl and his devotion to her. He would look at her and reminisce of the times they had spent together when she was a small child. She was truly very special to him and it showed in everything that he did. His concern for the cost of her wedding rang a bell as well since I have always been kind of, shall we say, frugal.

I was sitting there thinking about the day when I would be forced to come to terms with the same issues Martin was dealing with. Could I ever give her away to any man? He will have to be very exceptional and somehow worthy to be married to the most special woman in the whole world, my daughter. Later, I came to understand that the one thing that would make him worthy would be that she loved him and had chosen him to be the one with whom she wanted to spend the rest of her life. I also fantasized about all the terrible things that I would do to him if he ever hurt her. Then I caught myself and thought that I was worrying about something that was far, far away. I would have years to try to prepare for her getting married and in the meantime, I would just enjoy her teenage years.

What Happened to Yesterday?

Well, I am sorry to say that the time soon came when I discovered that those years had passed like minutes and I found myself intimately and anxiously involved in preparation for my daughter's wedding. It seemed like one minute I was on that plane watching Steve Martin suffer one anxiety attack after another. Now it was six years later and I **WAS** Steve Martin. The next few months would be busy to say the least…and expensive!

I had first thought that arranging for the preacher, buying a few flowers, and ordering some food would be easy enough. What was the big deal? Needless to say, after only a few weeks into the planning stage, I knew that this was going to be quite a bit more complicated than I had thought. I kept telling myself, "You only have one daughter!" That would help for a little while, but then I would learn what the string quartet would cost, or she would bring me the bill for the flowers. And then there was the wedding dress. And **WHAT A DRESS** it was! I could have paid a farmer to specially grow the cotton, a mill to weave it into the finest cloth, and a designer to draw hundreds of pictures until one appealed to my little girl. Then I could have hired the greatest seamstress to sew it together, and it couldn't have cost this much! What was she thinking? I am not a rich man. I have owned automobiles that didn't cost this much!

But then at some point I remember having a revelation that would change all of these anxious thoughts. "Who cares what it cost? This is my little girl's wedding." From that moment on, I was able to relax and, believe it or not, enjoy the whole ordeal.

Originally, we had decided to have it outdoors and at my place. I was busy building a gazebo, landscaping, while my daughter painted the bridge over the pond that she and I would cross. That would be her "aisle" for her most special walk. Flowers of just the right color were to be planted along the walkway and a complete remodel of my barn where the reception would take place was underway. There was so much to do and as time drew near, all were busy performing their assigned tasks. My sisters were extremely helpful doing the things that most men could never understand, much less actually pull off.

Plan " B "

October would be a good month for an outdoor wedding in Mississippi, we thought. It would be cooler outside and the weather, which can be unpredictable earlier in the tropical season, would have settled down by then. There was only one problem: September. It had been years since we had a hurricane in our area. But as it turned out, this would be the year and September would be the month. As I sat and watched the weather report on television, I could only think of the many hours of hard work and also the hundreds of dollars I had spent. As the storm approached, it was all in danger of being swept away.

Well, my premonition was right on target. All the work we had done in preparation for the wedding was either blown or washed away. Even the bridge that Casey had spent hours painting so meticulously white just wasn't there any more. The creek on which I live became a raging river washing away most things man-made in its path. When the water receded, not much was left of the wedding preparations. It would take two years to restore things to the way they had been before Hurricane Georges. A few days after the storm, I was surveying the immense damage with a sick feeling in the pit of my stomach. My home was only slightly damaged and for that I was grateful. But I had lost some old beloved friends…my trees. I stopped counting at 168 fallen, broken or uprooted trees of so many varieties. The prospect of just getting them cleaned up was enough to make me want to cry. Yet I was reminded that there was something more pressing and much more important.

It was decided that we would move the wedding to the church and I marveled as friends and relatives rallied around us in our efforts. From the very time the date for the wedding had been set, something had been bothering me. I had so many things that I wanted to say to my daughter as she was preparing to be married, but I couldn't seem to get them out. Mostly, I wanted to make sure, as she started her new life, that she knew how important she had always been to me. I was sure she knew something of how I felt about her, but I needed her to understand just how deeply I loved her. I sat at my computer for hours writing my thoughts and memories and not knowing what to do with them. Then, it came to me. I would somehow make them into a song. With the help of a friend who was musically gifted, I wrote a song that said all I needed to say for that moment in her life. I arranged for my nephew to sing it for her. I wanted this to be her most special day—one that she would always cherish. It would be a moment in her life that she could share someday with her own daughter.

The day of the wedding finally came and everyone was very busy, especially me. I was hurrying around the church working out one crisis after another and making final adjustments here and there. My two sisters had come the night before so that they could help with the last minute preparations. I remember thinking, "These two who were such a pain the neck when I was growing up sure do come in handy now." Actually, my sisters have always been there for me and I just can't imagine living my life without either of them. I have always been able to call on them when I needed the kind of comfort, love and acceptance that can only come from family. I owe each one of them far more than I can ever repay.

Here Comes the Bride

Eventually, guests started arriving and the string quartet began to play. It was time now to prepare to walk down the aisle. Casey came out in her wedding dress and I could not believe my eyes. For the first time, I saw my little girl as the wonderful mature woman that she was. At that moment she was the most beautiful woman I had ever seen in that gorgeous, (and **VERY EXPENSIVE**) wedding gown. I was so proud to be Casey's dad. But I was even more proud of the person she had become inside.

The wedding march started to play and we began our last walk together as a father and his unmarried daughter. She and I had taken so many walks together with her little three-year-old hand in mine. We continued these walks as that little hand grew larger and she grew taller. As the music played I thought back once more to the day I first held her in my arms. It had been twenty-one years...

twenty-one wonderful years of having the honor of being the father of this incredible bride. Nothing mattered anymore but the moment. All of the preparation, the expense and the guests were insignificant. They were all out of focus and I only saw her.

The only thoughts I had were of her at various stages of her life. Later, I would think it ironic that all of the things that had caused me such grief, the abandonment, the loneliness without her, the hurt…none of those things even came to mind at that moment. I could only think of good things. My mind went back to the times that I crawled around the living room for hours on my hands and knees with her riding on my back. I also remembered the many Saturdays when she was four and I would take her to work with me. I thought back to the fishing trips we made when she was around six to a little out of the way creek, just the two of us. What great times we used to have together. So many thoughts flooded my mind, all very happy, and all about my little girl.

Finally, we were at the altar and the preacher was speaking. He gave the usual introduction and then said that although this was a special day for the bride and groom, it was also a very special time for the parents as well. "Casey," he said, "because of his love for you, your Dad has a special gift at this time for you." Then, my nephew began to sing.

Look At You Now
"Look at you now, Casey…Look at you now.
I'm as proud as any father could ever be,
Caring for you, meant the world to me.
Oh, what times and fun we always had to share,
Beginning to sing, learning to talk,
Braiding your hair, and learning to walk,
Just look at you now, Casey.
I can still hear you hum that sweet little tune,
Just one more ride upon your knee please,

Daddy please?
First bike ride, driving the car,
I was right there by your side,
And look at you now,
Daddy's heart and joy and pride.
Oh, look at you now, coming down the aisle,
Hand in hand with the man of your dreams,
His beauty at his side.
A new life begun and one to unfold,
As you look to the future
And dream what it may hold,
Look at you now, Casey, look at you now.
Daddy's heart, his joy, his pride,
He's looking at the bride, my little girl
Casey, look at you now.

As I stood there beside my daughter, I felt her shaking as she began to weep. "Oh, no!" I thought, "I've made her cry again." Well at least these were tears of joy. She had gotten the message. I believe that in those few moments while her song was being sung, she came to realize the depth of my love for her. She knew that there would never be anyone, anywhere, at anytime who could ever take her place in my heart. She would always be her daddy's little girl and would be able to carry the memories of a father who loved her intensely throughout her life.

Suddenly, the song was over and the minister was asking who gives this woman in marriage? My answer was not rehearsed, it just came out. "Her mother and I." It was like there was no place anymore in my life for unforgiveness. This was just another way of telling her that she was more important than any issues I may ever have had in my life. I then kissed her on the cheek and turned, walked back to the second pew and sat beside her mother. It was at that very moment that I knew things would never be the same again. It was like I had been king in her life and my term was now up. The new guy was in the spotlight and

I was slipping unnoticed back into oblivion. In a few minutes she would have a husband and he would be her daily confidant. Would he be taking my place in her life? For these past few precious years, I had been the one she called when she had a problem with her car or when something went wrong at work. I didn't want to lose the contact with her that had taken so long to re-establish. It was a bittersweet time since I was happy for her and her new life yet knew how much I would miss the relationship we had together.

He Will Keep His Agreement of Love
Deuteronomy 7:9

It was also here that I became fully aware that God had answered my prayers. I had given my daughter to him to care for in my absence and he had done a wonderful job. But, he had also done for me what he did for Abraham. He had given her back and blessed me with several years with her, years filled with joy and happiness. These were not years where she lived with me and we interacted daily. No, that just wasn't to be. But there had come a time when she began to want to spend time with me again. It was as though things had come full circle and I was truly the beneficiary. She would call me from time to time or I would call her. We would talk catching up on what she had been doing and what had happened in my life. Many times we would decide to go out to dinner together and spend a couple of hours reminiscing or just talking about things that interested us. I was more thankful for these precious hours than anyone could know. They were small pieces of heaven and precious gifts from God. He had truly been faithful and I would love him all the more for it.

After months of planning and preparation, it was all over in a matter of minutes. She was kissing her new husband and the new love of her life. As they turned to walk back down the aisle as husband and wife, I could see in her eyes the incredible happiness resulting from a little girl's dream finally coming true. I had always wanted the best for her and this truly was her moment. She would belong to another now, but she would never cease to be the most important woman in my life. To me, she could never be anyone BUT...daddy's little girl.

At the reception, I watched her as though I might never see her again. She and her proud husband talked and laughed with the guests and occasionally, she would turn looking my way and smile that beautiful smile as if to say, "Thank you Daddy. I love you."

My happy, beaming smile spoke a heartfelt reply: "I love you too, Casey. "

10

If I Had it to Do all Over Again

I Need A Time Machine

"If only I could go back..." How many times have we said this to ourselves? Well, we can't. What has happened, has happened and we will have to deal with the consequences.

We cannot change anything we have done, no matter how much we may regret it. However, we can learn from our experiences. Somewhere through my own ordeal, I was made to understand something that would drastically alter my perspective forever. I came to realize that children tend to be very selfish. I'm not being critical when I say that. It's just a fact. They are outspoken about what they want and when they want it. Most of the time their entire focus is on what will make them happy and nothing else. They have not yet learned the importance of considering the needs and feelings of others as well as their own. In a family environment where mother and dad are still married and living with the children, this behavior, though certainly bothersome, can usually be tolerated; it is in fact what is normally to be expected. After all they are just children, right?

When a parent is placed into a non-custodial role, these dynamics change significantly. Suddenly, the selfish behavior of the child looms much larger and appears to be quite out of proportion. That parent may think, "I am the one who is no longer in the loop, I am the one who has been robbed of precious time with my child, I am the one who suffers from the injustice of the situation. This child should recognize these things and help me through all of this." Oh, you may not say this out loud, or even think it consciously, but subconsciously, probably everyone in this situation feels this way.

Even the custodial parent tends to focus on this natural selfishness of the child. Being under the daily pressures of maintaining a home, working, cooking, dealing with financial matters, helping the child with homework, shopping, and so many other things, one begins to feel overwhelmed. When the child fails to respond the way the parent thinks he should, sometimes that will light the fuse for what will eventually be an exploding bomb. Again this parent might say, "What's wrong with this kid? Can't he see that I am under a lot of pressure and that I need his support. I am doing the job of a mother and father and no one appreciates it, especially my child." Does this sound familiar to anyone?

So each parent feels pressured for one reason or another. Each one also may think that he or she is being treated unfairly by the ex-spouse, the child, and possibly even the justice system. They can't always take out their frustrations on the ex-spouse, and it would never serve any purpose to scream at the judge. That just leaves one person—the child. Picture two large kids on the playground with a smaller one in between them. They begin yelling at the small kid and one pushes him. The other big kid pushes him back in the other direction, and this goes on and on. Do you see now how much this resembles the situation of the child of a divorce that has to deal with two angry, frustrated, and hurt parents?

Hey! I'm Just a Kid!

One doesn't stop being a child just because the parents divorce. We do our children a grave injustice when we expect them to grow up prematurely in the name of helping us cope with our problems. We have a tendency to ask them to do things we wouldn't ask thirty-year-old adults to do, all just to make ourselves feel better. If we Americans are bent on marrying, having children, and divorcing, then we need at least to learn to treat our children like children. I wish I could tell you that I had responded to my daughter correctly in every situation. Quite the contrary, I blew it more times than I can remember.

I am standing on the other side now and looking back. What I see is a dad who made many mistakes with his child and, in hindsight, I can see that it didn't have to be that way. It comes down to admitting one huge weakness that took over and ruled the way I thought and the way that I treated her. That weakness was selfishness. It is a very natural thing for us to be selfish. We are born with an instinct for self-preservation. As we grow older, we become more aware of the needs of others and hopefully, less focused on our own. Through these years of growing into a young adult, we struggle with a natural dilemma; will we do what is best for ourselves or consider and respond to the needs of others? When a crisis appears, such as our divorce, many times we regress to self-preservation once more.

When we begin to really be honest with ourselves, we will conclude that the cause of most of the mistakes we make which aren't the result of ignorance or misinformation, is selfishness. Choosing the wrong mate can be a selfish thing to do. It may have been that you wanted that person for yourself and you wanted her or him right then. You didn't want to wait until the infatuation or passion wore off so that you could see clearly. The use and abuse of drugs and alcohol is also an act of selfishness. When we choose substance abuse, we are in essence saying, "I want to feel good now...I want to feel good about myself now. I will do whatever is necessary to make that happen." And so it stands to reason that if we make mistakes with our children as we are attempting to deal with a divorce, the reason could also be due to our selfishness.

It is very important for us to recognize our tendency to be selfish, for when we do, we can make a conscious effort to think of the needs of the child and not just our own. In fact, this is the litmus test. We should ask ourselves why we want this child to do this or that. Is it for the child's best interest or our own? Many times, if we are honest, we may not like the answer.

It is also because of selfishness, that our children sometimes are neglected. A single mother might say, "I have lived my whole life for someone else. Now it's my turn." The result of that attitude may be dating a lot of men, or just going out a lot. Occasionally, it may involve throwing herself into a career. In either case, the children suffer as a result of this kind of selfishness. Not only have they lost a parent from the home, but the one who still lives with them may be gone a lot as well and they are left to be raised by daycare centers, school teachers, and baby sitters.

There are those in places of influence that preach a doctrine of focusing on ourselves. These not only condone putting our children in daycare, but they encourage it. This puts the needs of the parents first. Of course, there are those situations where childcare is the only option. But the ultimate goal should always be to bring the child back under the constant care of a loving parent as quickly as possible. This is an ongoing dilemma with a loving custodial parent who recognizes the need to be significantly influential in the daily upbringing of the child.

On the other hand, a non-custodial parent might say, "I have been shut out of the lives of my family and treated unfairly. Now, I will create a new life just for me." Here, he may find another wife with kids of her own and take them for his new family. Within these circumstances, there may be a tendency to spend less and less time with his own child. The new wife expects him to take on the responsibilities of a father to her children and since they live with him, they get more of his attention. More times than not, when this occurs it is very easy to alienate himself totally from his own kids in a very short period of time. It is easier for him to just focus on those in his house. It is a lot of work to keep up the visitation regimen with his own children. And yet there are many non-custodial parents who strive to stay in the loop; doing everything possible to maintain, and even continue to improve their relationship with their children.

Selfishness is a destroyer of relationships. Our relationships should be sacred to us, especially our relationship with our children. I am convinced that should we choose to put a very high value on these relationships with others, most conflicts, hurts, and many divorces would be avoided.

" I Hate Divorce!" God

Looking back, I can see that I have learned a lot, but the most profound lesson came after many years of reflection. Yet it has been a wonderful insight and has caused me to reorder many areas of my life. You see, God hates divorce. Why do I believe that? I believe it because I have seen how much pain and suffering it inflicts on everyone involved, especially the children. And I believe it because there are passages in the Bible that explicitly say so. Malachi 2:16 says, *"I hate divorce, says the Lord God of Israel."* Do you need further proof? If so, look at Matthew 19:3-9 and Mark 10:2-12 and others. Even though he hates it, he also sometimes allows it, for example in cases involving adultery. I am also convinced that God can empathize in a very special way with the plight of the non-custodial parent.

It eventually occurred to me that in a very important sense God, our Father, is a non-custodial parent. Since we are not physically with him, we may very often leave him out of the loop in our own life. Just as the child can be selfish, not realizing the hurts and needs of the non-custodial parent, we too can be selfish toward our Heavenly Father. Do we refuse to visit him regularly or to allow him to visit us? Do we decline to let him be a part of our daily routine, failing to consult him with our problems as we should? How often, if at all, do we remember to tell him how much we love him?

I was feeling very sorry for myself one weekend because my daughter refused to spend time with me, and I was all alone. As I engaged in a marathon of self-pity, it finally struck me: God must feel sad and lonely sometimes too, because of my refusal to visit and spend time with him. How often had I made promises to him, and then broken them because something else that seemed more appealing came along? Many times I had felt slighted and hurt when my daughter chose to do something that I felt was trivial instead of spending time with me. I must have made God feel the same way for equally trivial reasons many times?

He had given me gifts that he wanted me to have...special gifts from his heart only to see me turn my nose up at them because they were not what I wanted. Instead, I sought after things that were more attractive to me. He never failed to support me and provide for my needs. Everything I ever really needed was there and I consistently took it for granted. Yet through all of this, he was always my perfect Father. He never gave up, never yelled at me and never made me feel worthless. He never turned his back on me, trading me in on a new kid. He was always there fighting for his time with me...fighting for his visitation.

Scripture teaches that he has empathy with us and that could only be true if he has experienced the same feelings that we have. As I was feeling so low and sorry for myself, it was like I sensed him to say, "Yes, I know. I understand." In a silent but real exchange, I thought, "How could you? You're God." In his still small voice, he impressed upon me that as hurt and abandoned as I had felt, he had experienced the same thing many times from all of his children ...and yes, even from me. My feelings of abandonment paled as compared to his. I was dealing with one child and for a few short years. He had been fighting for his time with his millions upon millions of children for thousands of years...beginning with Adam. This was the lesson that came from this time in my life, which turned out to be the greatest lesson of my whole life.

What to Change

If I had it all to do over again, would I do things differently? You bet I would! To begin with, I would try even harder than I did not to involve my child in the divorce process, and would do everything in my power to see to it that others didn't either. It seems that when we are hurt, we lose our sense of good judgment and common sense. In such situations we will do things that we normally would not even consider. Sometimes in the name of righteousness, we take a stand to do the "right thing", but that often turns out to mean the "selfish thing". Looking back, I realize that things would have been so much better for all of us if I had agreed to the joint custody compromise that I had been offered. However, in my clouded judgment, I wanted total control of the environment in which my daughter would be raised—all or (practically) nothing.

I have often wondered what it would have been like if I had chosen joint custody. In the first place, the circumstances that resulted in my daughter's first choosing to live with me and then later changing that choice to go with her mother would have been avoided. This alone would have been a very good thing. Another advantage would have been that our family secrets (the personal aspects of our marriage) would not have been aired, and the venting of bitter feelings might have been averted. In a custody battle, it seems that no restraints apply, and people will stop at nothing to get their way. Secrets known only to husband and wife, things shared in confidence, become public knowledge, and even become weapons with which to destroy the character of the adversarial spouse. Those original promises to *"love, and to cherish....till death do us part,"* suddenly are transformed into a determination to *"hate, and to detest .... till death do us part and the sooner the better."* Are not these the same two persons who could not stand to be apart for even a few hours and could not wait to get home to each other after a day's work? Now they seem so emotionally enraged that they are willing to say or do anything they can think of to hurt and degrade each other. It is hard to imagine wanting to inflict such spite and hurt on anyone, much less on the person who, above all others, you so recently loved. Perhaps if I had chosen joint custody, much of this could have been avoided.

Finally, one other thing I would change is that I would focus totally on my daughter and what is in her best interest. I would weigh every word that I spoke, every act, even every gesture. With each one, I would ask "what effect will this have on her?" If it meant losing a battle, being intimidated, embarrassed or appearing to be the fool, that would be a small price to pay for her welfare. Instead, I did many things wrong, things directed to my own self-interest rather than to her well being.

The Magic Ingredient

One right thing that I did was to cover her with prayer. I believe that God protected her mind and her emotional well being from my mistakes as a direct answer to my prayers for her. What justifies my making such a claim? It is very evident, despite having to live through the divorce of her parents, that my daughter is one of the most well-adjusted young women that I have ever known. She appears to be completely unaffected by anything that might have been done which could have had a harmful affect on her. I am ever so grateful that the Lord preserved her throughout this whole ordeal.

If I had it to do over again, I would do practically everything differently. But what would I not change? She never doubted that her dad wanted her with him. She has never had to deal with the abandonment of a parent and as far as I am concerned, she never will. My heart breaks when I see the hurt brought upon a child that the parent considers to be too much trouble. I am completely amazed and saddened when I see a non-custodial father choose to move away from his child for employment purposes or any other reason when it may not be absolutely necessary. When a child's parent remarries and inherits a new family, I can imagine the feelings of abandonment that the biological children must feel. Then, when this parent begins to spend less and less time with his kid in favor of his new family, just think of the feelings of rejection the child must carry. I am very aware that remarriages occur and in many cases, the children of divorce are not only considered, but are well cared for and given the love and attention that they deserve. But unfortunately, in far too many of these blended families, this just isn't the case.

Have you ever decided that an automobile was no longer suitable and decided to trade it in on a new one? What about clothing that has gone out of style and just hangs in your closet never being worn? Remember that old sofa that you loved so much when you purchased it? Now it has been replaced by a new one and off it goes to the Salvation Army. Are you beginning to get the picture? The automobile, the clothing and the sofa do not have feelings. Your child does. You may ask, "Don't I deserve to have a life?" You do, but not at the expense of your child. Sometimes when you choose to "have a life," you also may be choosing to destroy the life of your child. Be very careful, parent.

Once the disciples came to Jesus and asked Him, *"Who is the greatest in the kingdom of heaven?"* Jesus called a little child over and set him in the middle of them and said, *"Whosoever therefore shall humble himself as this little child, the same is greatest in the kingdom of heaven. And whoso shall receive one such little child in my name receiveth me. But whoso shall offend one of these little ones which believe in me; it were better for him that a millstone were hanged about his neck, and that he were drowned in the depth of the sea."*

And so, I urge every parent to listen carefully to these words from the Bible. It is my belief that many will stand before God and have to answer as to why they traded their child for "a life." You might say, "God doesn't expect me to put my life on hold until my child is grown?" This is my question to you: "What is more important to you than your child?" I suggest that your answer should be, "Nothing; absolutely nothing." If this is your answer, then God might expect you to put your life on hold while you take care of your parental responsibility. What is quite clear is this: the parent's effort to "have a life" must not override his or her duty to the child.

Good Medicine Taste Bad

These are words that many divorced parents do not want to hear. It is only natural to have the dream of re-establishing yourself in every way. That includes another mate and children at home that you can have a direct input in their upbringing. It is natural, but it doesn't excuse the shirking of parental responsibility to your own child who is not living with you. As I said earlier, over the years since my divorce and while my daughter was still a minor, I had a couple of romantic relationships. Although my daughter was approving of these relationships, she always knew that she was still first. I assured her that I would never marry anyone who would not be compatible with our father / daughter relationship. She has been disappointed in me for not marrying someone she liked. I believe that she had this attitude because she never felt threatened. No one would ever take her place in my life and she knew that.

What about you Dad? What about you Mom? Does your little girl or your little boy know that she or he is first with you? If that hasn't been the case in the past, it's not too late. Children are very forgiving and ready to begin again when you are. "Blood is thicker than water." You participated in creating that precious little miracle; he or she is your responsibility and will be, until the child becomes an adult. You cannot delegate that to a stepparent and shame on you if you try. Please go call him or her right now and make plans to become more involved than ever in that dear little life.

What would I do if I had it to do over again? I would love her more, be with her more, talk to her more and be a better dad than anyone, any place, any time. It would not only be my responsibility, but it would be my privilege.

11

Joy Comes In the Morning

Learning to Live when We'd Rather Die

It has been proven that the more stress a person is under, the more questionable that person's decisions will be. To make good choices, to decide what is best for all involved, we need to remove ourselves from the heat of the moment and allow some time to think clearly. Although receiving information and advice from others can be very helpful, there are also times when we need to be apart from it. We need to find a special place where we can reflect on our situation—a quiet place where we can hear God's voice. My special place is very similar to the one I had as a child.

I have always enjoyed walking in the woods alone. Here, I can take time to think, smell the various scents of the outdoors and observe the fascinating things going on around me. I watch for squirrels and other animals. When I see one I will stop to see what it will do. I also like to look at the trees. They are all unique and each one seems to be telling its own story. Some are bent in an unnatural way showing the effect that a storm might have had on them in years past. Some are extremely tall and healthy, which indicates that they weathered those same storms and continued to flourish and reach for the sky. Others are dead; they are still standing, but have no life in them at all. As I reflected on all of this, I determined that people are like trees. Some are bent and scarred by the storms of life. Others stand tall and healthy spreading forth their branches proudly and beautifully. Then there are those who, though still standing, seem to have no life left in them. They have lost their joy and are producing no fruit and no shade for the weary.

Life can be the best and life can be the worst, but either way it beats the alternative. Some people who are experiencing some very deep dark valleys in their lives might argue with this. Right now, your life may be filled with hurt, loneliness, anger and perhaps even a feeling of abandonment. But it is important to remember that whatever you may be experiencing at the moment is temporary. There is one thing you can be certain of and that is, things are ever changing. It may seem as though you are trapped in a revolving door and can't get out. At times like that, and as hard as it might be, a person just has to be patient.

There are some things that can make your life seem the very best all of the time. Good health, never experiencing a loss, always being gainfully employed, only knowing and associating with honest and trustworthy people—all these things and countless others would make your life more enjoyable, more palatable. But have you ever thought about just how boring it would be if everything went well all the time? Our lives would be shallow, superficial, and we wouldn't be able to appreciate just how great life is when we are not in the valley, but rather standing on the mountain top and savoring God's creation.

These bad experiences can be the character builders that turn ordinary people into the extraordinary, the experienced, the proven, and the wise. The end result is someone who can be useful to others and who is able to give invaluable advice to those who may be headed for disaster. Occasionally, someone may even choose to heed that advice and be spared as a result.

Wet Shoes ... Warm Heart

One of the greatest and most memorable movies of all time, in my opinion, was *"Singing in the Rain,"* starring the great Gene Kelly. I remember as a child going to the theater and seeing this movie when it was relatively new. Later, my second grade teacher chose it as the theme for a play for her class to perform. She worked very hard teaching us our parts and directing our pitiful acting skills. For some reason, which I cannot remember, I was selected to sing the title song. As I look back, I can't imagine why I agreed to do it. I also can't believe I ever managed to find the courage to pull it off. Nevertheless, I did. We didn't have back up tapes and for some reason there was not a piano player, so we had to improvise. I had a second cousin who had the unique talent of being able to whistle without puckering. Our classmates were always fascinated with that and would gather around her at recess to try to figure out how she did it. Someone suggested that she accompany me by whistling as I sang.

Finally, the day came and we were on stage in front of an auditorium full of students, teachers, and parents. As I sang *"Singing In The Rain"*, the audience was bewildered trying to figure out who was whistling since none of the kids were puckered up. Even today when I see a clip from that movie and watch Gene Kelly dancing with his umbrella and splashing in the puddles in the street, I laugh and think about that day when I was a singing star with my whistling backup. Who knows, maybe that was my fifteen minutes of fame. If so, at least I got it over with at an early age.

You know, there was a great lesson in that old movie. Though the producers may not have intended this, they did show everyone that it is possible to sing in the rain. No matter how bad things seem to be, we can still choose to be happy. We have within us the ability to weather the storms that come our way and to love life. Here it comes again, but I have to say it. **It is a choice!** We also have the choice to wallow in our self-pity while we live out a miserable existence. But if we will just make the effort we can choose to love life even during the trials and hardships. Is that to say that we will never be sad, never depressed, discouraged or frustrated? Of course not, but we do not have to camp out with these emotions and make them a part of our everyday life.

The greatest book ever written has a few things to say about this. In Psalms 126 verse 5, it says *"Those who sow in tears will reap with songs of joy."* Also, Psalms 30 verse 5 says, *"Weeping may endure for a night, but joy cometh in the morning."* Each day is brand new and comes to us with a clean slate on which we may write its own new story. Many times I chose to allow a new day to be just a time when the troubles of the days past would repeat themselves. But eventually, I learned how to stop the negatives and replace them with positives. That's when I began to learn to *"sing in the rain."*

It's not always easy, but it is definitely worth the effort. It has been said that "life is 10 percent what we make it and 90 percent how we take it." Have you ever seen someone who has experienced many awful trials, yet that person remains positive and happy through them all? For many years, I couldn't understand this. In fact, I thought they must have been faking it. Now I know that it is possible to be this way even when things are really bad.

But How?

For me, I had to face several facts that were crucial to choosing joy through trials. These were:

1. Looking to the future and envisioning it as better than the past is essential to maintaining a positive attitude. Dwelling on past achievements or failures is usually non-productive and can many times cause us to drift into depression. I determined that I would not allow myself to focus on the negative events of the past.

2. I would stay busy doing things that were worthwhile. First, I worked very hard and diligently in my career. Second, I decided to begin to build friend-

ships with people who would lift me up rather than cause me to doubt. Finally, I would devote a large portion of my time to serving the Lord. I continued to teach a Bible study class, but I also sought God's guidance as to other avenues of ministry he might open up to me.

3. I would continue to remind myself to keep things in their proper perspective. Although life as we know it is important, sometimes I think we lose sight of how it ranks as compared to eternity. From God's perspective, problems that seem insurmountable to us probably appear trivial. This life is but a vapor while eternity is forever.

What's Around the Corner?

I believe that there is one other key ingredient to choosing joy through trials. What if, as you were experiencing one of your darkest moments, you could look into the future and see that eventually, everything was not only going to just be alright, but better than anyone could imagine? Sure, you will have to suffer for a while, but as you see your future, you realize that your current problem is but another step on the stairway to happiness. As you read what follows, you may begin to understand what I mean.

I confess to you that I find it hard to read mystery novels. There is one main reason. I never can resist the temptation once the crime is discovered, to flip over to the last chapter to see who did it. But once I know, what is the purpose of reading all of those chapters in between? And so, I am finished with the book after reading only two chapters, the first and the last. The situation is much different when reading the Bible. In the first few chapters of this greatest book of all time, we see a crime committed. It involved Adam and Eve and their disobedience of God. Then, in the final chapters of the Bible, we see the real villain exposed and watch as he gets his much deserved punishment. But unlike the usual mystery novel, the Bible contains vital information that cannot be overlooked in all those books in between.

The book of Revelation does reveal one important fact that helped me most of all. It shows that ultimately we win! That took a lot of the suspense and much of the anxiety out of life for me. No matter what happens, when things get really bad, when people disappoint me, and when my very existence seems to be threatened, I know that the battle is already won. Christ fought it for us at the cross. He endured awful shame, inhumane torture, agony beyond our imaginations, and ultimately, after a long, cruel crucifixion, death. Why? So we could be at peace and live with him in eternity forever. He did all of this so we could live in victory in this life right here and now. All of this...so that we could *"sing in the rain."*

" I Can See Clearly Now, the Rain Has Gone "

Now, standing on the other side of what I thought was the most awful time of my life, I have a perfect view of the past and can see what I did not see at the time. Now, as I look back, I can see that I wasn't in it alone. Oh, I had a competent attorney, two pastor friends who were there for me even in court and of course a wonderful, loyal and loving family. But now I see that the same one I have mentioned so many times before, was also there with me every step of the way. Now I can see the way he worked in the details and how he comforted me when I was anxious. He promised that *"He would never leave me nor forsake me."* Indeed, he never has, neither then nor now. It is ironic that when Jesus was experiencing his darkest moment, there was no one there for him. His disciples ran away, and he even felt that God, the Father, had turned his back on him. Yet he has promised always to be there for his children. The one who was abandoned on the cross has promised never to abandon his own.

We have all heard the phrase, *"resting in the Lord"* most

of our lives. It is a phrase that seems to lose its meaning after so much use. But because of something that happened to me one summer when I was a young teenager, I now know exactly what it means.

I was spending the summer at our fishing camp. One of my friends came to stay several days with me. We would ride in my old boat for hours at a time. As we traveled up the river for miles, occasionally we would stop at a sandbar to swim. One day, when it had been raining and the river was dangerously swift, we pulled up to a sand bar for a rest. My friend was very athletic and in fact, he eventually went on to play quarterback for the Green Bay Packers. He decided that we should swim the river. Well, it was very wide, deep and swift at that particular place. I had always respected the river, never challenging it to a duel. I knew that I had my limits but I was sure that the river had none. He dived in and yelled at me to follow. What could I do? I jumped in behind him and immediately I could feel the strong current and sensed the immeasurable strength of the bloated river. By the time I was about halfway across, I had become very tired. There was a moment when I had the thought that I might not make it. It was then that I decided to just relax. I rolled over on my back and began to float. I was amazed at the ease with which I floated to the other side.

Life can be like that swollen river, full of fury and bullying its way through time as it threatens to swallow up anyone who would try to get across it to the other side. There are times when we want to swim upstream trying to defy the swift current, fighting a battle we can never win. Sad to say, some actually don't make it and are victims of life's ruthless undertow. They are taken under by it and drown as they struggle to reach the top. But, there are others who learn the secret that I learned that day. These have learned to relax and to allow the very thing that would destroy them to move them toward their ultimate destination.

In much the same way, I have learned the true meaning of *"resting in the Lord."* He, like the river, can hold us up and carry us if we can only learn to relax, trust him, and to rest in him. The key is trust. It wasn't natural for me to trust that deep and swift river, but once I was faced with a choice of trust it or sink and die, I chose to calm myself, relax and float to the other side. Many people, when faced with the trials of life, choose to continue to struggle. Eventually, they wear themselves out, and drown. Some give up completely, making no effort at all, and also drown. They have become overwhelm by life and its troubles. At the very least, they have allowed their problems to rob them of the joy of living. Trusting is an unnatural act that has to be learned which usually takes considerable effort.

Catch Me ... Please?

My daughter and I devised a little game when she was very small that she called "the trust game." She would stand very stiff with her arms straight down by her side and close her eyes. I would position myself behind her and tell her to slowly fall backward. "Go ahead Baby," I would say, "Trust Daddy. I will always catch you." Well, at first, she would begin leaning back and just as she would start to lose her balance, she would move one foot backwards to regain her balance catching herself. She wanted so badly to trust me and enjoy the blind fall back into her daddy's arms but it wasn't easy for her. Slowly but surely, and over time, she came to trust me totally and completely to catch her...and I always did. We played this game even into her teens and she wouldn't even flinch, just fall back into my arms with total and complete trust for her daddy. It's difficult to describe how wonderful that made me feel. To earn the complete trust of someone you care so deeply for, is like receiving an award for winning a very lengthy endurance contest. There is incredible satisfaction as you finally cross the finish line.

God wants us to trust him in this very way, closing our eyes and falling back into the arms of our heavenly Father. This is the greatest compliment we can pay him. By doing this, we show him that we know he is capable of doing what he has told us he will do. We also demonstrate that we recognize his immeasurable love for us. I would have died before I would have allowed my daughter fall and hurt herself. Not only that, but if I had let her fall even once, she may not ever have trusted me again. That would have been my worst nightmare. God loves us much more than we could ever love our children. It follows that he would be even more careful to protect the trust we would demonstrate toward him. Casey's trusting me in this way thrilled me and made me proud to be her dad. Resting in him makes God a very happy Father, one who might say, *"This is my child in whom I am well pleased."*

I am reminded of a made-for-TV movie about a Mafia boss and his family. There was a scene where his little boy was standing high up on a wall and the father told him to jump and he would catch him. The little boy was torn, wanting so badly to put his trust in his dad and yet at the same time, very reluctant. Eventually, the child gave in and jumped deciding that his dad knew best. The father moved back very deliberately and allowed his son to fall onto the ground and get hurt. He told his son, "Let that be a lesson to you to never trust anyone". I'm sure his son did learn a lesson that day and it was all about a cold and very hard parent. Can you imagine the impact that this had on that little boy? Everyone needs someone to trust, someone that we can depend on and come to when we have a real need. To take this away from a child is not only cruel; I believe it also to be immoral.

In maybe a less dramatic way, a parent may fail to show up for his child's sporting event, a play, maybe a pageant or recital. The effect is the same. Being there for what is important to your children is much like catching them when they jump, or as in my daughter's case, when she falls back into daddy's arms. There is nothing you will ever do that will be more important than earning and deserving your child's trust. Even being late for a child's function speaks volumes to the young ones. I can remember as a second grader looking into the audience at the school auditorium the day I sang *"Singing In The Rain"* and finding my mother sitting out there. How happy I was to see her. I would have felt very badly if she had not been there that day. Yes ... she got that one right. It was my dad who wasn't there.

I will never forget the lesson that I learned as I swam that river. I made it across that day and never felt that it was necessary to try that again. But should the occasion ever present itself and I was forced to make that treacherous crossing again, I now know the secret. I also know the *Peacemaker*. And I know how to trust.

12

Airborne

Flying High While Thinking Low

As a young child and even as an adolescent, I had two favorite pastimes. The first was climbing. I loved to climb and have been yelled at many times by my grandmother telling me to come down from the top of nearly every tree on their property. My grandfather was much easier on me though, recognizing it as a "boy thing." He also saw that I was good at it and when I was older he paid me to climb his pecan trees and shake the limbs so the nuts would fall to the ground. Then, he or people he would hire would pick them up and he would sell them.

I loved heights and I would climb anything. Though my favorite was trees, I also climbed onto the roof of our house, my grandfather's barn, my dad's shop, and anything else that was high. When I was up there, I felt big, special, and free. The other great thing about it was that things looked different from up there. As you can tell from what I have written, I didn't always like the way things looked at ground level. There were many complications; lots of problems for a child like me down there. When I was climbing high up, I was above all of that, alone and at peace.

My other favorite pastime was lying flat on my back on the ground and looking up at the sky. I had several places where I liked to do this. One was way out in my grandfather's pasture. There were no obstructions, nothing to interfere with my view of the clouds as they slowly passed over. The other favorite place was at school. Many times at recess, I would wander slightly off school property and lie down under the pine trees on the soft pine straw. I can still hear the wind as it blew through the pines and remember wishing that I was in the very tops of those tall trees. Or, better yet, I would wish that I could soar like the graceful birds I would watch flying above. The sky seemed to be alluring and it felt to me like it must be so much better up there.

Soaring Above All Troubles

The home that I built for my wife and I was a few blocks from a small community airport. While working in the yard, I would hear the small planes above and stop to watch as they flew over. One day I was outside when a plane came over and I began wondering who was flying it and where he was going? What was he feeling and more important, what was he seeing? It was then that I made up my mind. I would start taking flying lessons and experience it for myself.

Before long I had enrolled in flying school and was sitting in the left seat of a Cessna 150. The flight instructor was a nice young man who seemed to know everything about airplanes and flying. It was extremely intimidating to me, but I sure was not going to admit it. Sitting there with many mixed emotions, I opened the throttle and off we went down the bumpy runway. In seconds I reached the magic speed for takeoff and I pulled back on the yoke. Suddenly, the small plane carrying the instructor and me was airborne. We climbed higher and higher as he gave me instructions in a very calm manner. I made a very wide circle and headed back for the airport. Now it was time to land and I wasn't sure that I was up to it. I was still very nervous about the takeoff and needed time to get over that. But with the instructor right there by my side and giving me specific instructions in a soft but firm voice, the landing turned out to be a piece of cake.

That first day, I was so nervous I don't remember taking in any of the scenery from up there. But before long,

I was flying solo and really enjoying the view. Nothing looked the same as it did on the ground. Streets that seemed to be long and wide from ground level, were short and narrow from up there. Homes that were very large and expensive looked much like those that were small and inexpensive. The tall trees were as small bushes and automobiles like miniatures. All my life I had longed to soar like the birds and now I was doing it. Up there I had only one enemy and that was gravity. Flight is very temporary and eventually gravity will bring you down.

I remember flying over my house and thinking how peaceful it looked from up there. I thought, "I know all of its secrets." Then it occurred to me that every house I saw from high above their rooftops had some secrets as well. When we are having problems in our families, we have a tendency to think that we are the only one and wish we could be happy like everyone else. The truth is, most families have problems from time to time. It may seem that their problems aren't as serious as ours because when it's happening to us, there is nothing more important or more critical. As I looked down on the rooftops, I remember thinking that each home had a story to tell, "if their walls could only talk."

Cautiously Joyful

Flying was wonderful, yet with a few exceptions. As great as I have made it sound, there were some problems with my flying. First, I was always conscious of certain obstructions in the air. I had a fear of getting too low and flying into a radio tower. I had read a story once about a small plane much like the one I was flying hitting a very tall radio tower in Florida. That was the bad news, the good news was that it lodged at the top of the tower and the pilot somehow survived. I figured that the odds of that happening again were next to none and should that happen to me, well…let's just say that I was very careful to stay above typical tower heights. I also remember my first cross-country flight. My instructor became disoriented and for a brief time, we were lost and in the dark. I knew that if I had been alone when that happened, I couldn't possibly have figured out where I was. Then, there was always the possibility of hitting another plane in mid air.

Quite often, I would be flying and would remember a problem at work, or something that needed attention around the house. Someone would come to mind that I had not seen in a while and it would occur to me that I should call him. I began to realize that although escaping up into the sky above might be an intriguing thing to do, reality needs my constant attention. There are only two realms of reality: the one we are now living, and that one we look forward to living in eternally in the world to come. Man hasn't made a flying machine that can carry us through into that second realm. If we are to enter it, it must be through faith in Jesus Christ who has been called the *"Door"* and *"the Way, the Truth, and the Life."* Christ said of himself, *"No man comes to the Father but by me."* No plane, or even a space ship can bring us through into that eternal realm. We enter through the one who said he was *"going to prepare a place for us, so that where he is we may be also."*

This time in my life when I was flying was also a crucial time for my business. It seemed that there were never enough hours in the day to accomplish the things that needed attention. I had never been one to take up a hobby like golf or fishing and enjoy it for very long since I usually found myself thinking of more important things that I should be doing. With flying, I had accomplished what I had set out to do. I had soared far above the trees and into the clouds. I had taken off in a plane all alone and brought it back safely many times. Now it was time to land for good and take care of business.

As a young boy climbing trees or lying down and looking up at the sky, escaping was a luxury I could afford.

Now, I was a grown man with a family and matters that only I could address. These couldn't be resolved from up there. I never flew a plane again and I have never missed it. The real excitement is right here on the ground and there's plenty of it. Life can certainly be a struggle, but it is also quite an exciting ride. I will be *"airborne"* again someday in a much different way, but until then, I will be dealing with the issues of this life at slightly above sea level.

Priorities

For all of us, those issues should include being responsible, godly parents to our children. Many parents seem to have their heads in the clouds while they trample on their own children. Some have their boats, golf, hunting trips, sports bars, or even their careers and then, everything else comes next. There are those who put their children in daycare so they can have their own space. Sorry, but your space and your children's space should be one and the same. When we delegate the job of raising our children to a baby sitter or daycare center, one thing is certain. The child will recognize that he or she is not as important as whatever you choose to do in lieu of being with him or her. I do realize that there are cases where this may be a necessary evil. Many single mothers, in particular, struggle to earn a living for themselves and their children. They may have no alternative but to use daycare. Although this may be necessary, it shouldn't be looked upon as a permanent solution to caring for her child. Many employers are now allowing single mothers the opportunity to work at home. Also, other single moms are being creative by starting home-based businesses and being with their children as they work at home.

Although it may be necessary to use childcare, we must also expect there to be a price to pay; and it will usually be our children who will pay it. As a result of this thirty plus year-old trend, we now have what appears to be an entire generation of people with what many identify as self-esteem problems. Parents delegating their duties to anyone else can make a child feel that he or she is dispensable, unimportant. The result can sometimes be behavioral problems.

Parenting for me when I was a child was delegated to my grandparents. As I said earlier, we lived in a small town and it seemed that everyone knew our business. As a young boy and adolescent, I never felt adequate. I was embarrassed in school about the conduct of my mother and father, although compared to what we see parents doing today, I guess they weren't so bad after all. I had never heard of low self-esteem, I just knew that I felt that I wasn't as good as other people. My sisters and I were routinely dropped off at my grandparents' home while my parents went off to "enjoy themselves." As a child, I longed to spend time with them, but it seemed as though it wasn't reciprocal. I cannot remember my dad ever playing catch with me or even sitting on the porch talking as fathers and sons should. I can't imagine what I would have done had my father come to me and put his arm around my shoulders and said, "Let's take a walk, son." I would probably have thought that he was going to tell me something very bad.

" Listen My Son and You Shall Hear "

I was a quiet kid and I learned at an early age the advantages of listening. I was like a little sponge soaking up everything I heard and this has proven to be a great asset in my life. In my later years, I have observed that the art of listening seems to be an endangered one. Most of us have views on every subject and ours is always the correct one, right? Well, as a little guy I would just listen to everyone talk about all kinds of things, and would seldom contribute to the conversation. I would just sit there taking in and storing data.

I can recall wishing I were more outgoing. I would

admire those who were always talking, laughing and drawing attention to themselves. But some of the people I grew up with who were like that and were deemed by everyone who knew them as "most likely to succeed", seem to have burned out. It's as if they had shared all they knew and because they weren't good listeners, were not taking in new information to share. Some of the introverts went on to do significant things making an impact in one way or another.

Listening is definitely an art and I think I must have mastered it as a young boy. I feel very strongly about this, I think that the craft of listening should be taught in school—if it could be.

Because of this quiet and reserved personality that I had as a child, I am attracted to kids who are that way. I will pick them out of a crowd and try to spend time with them. I remember once when I was a youth worker in our church, I chaperoned a youth retreat at a camp out of town. I noticed one young lady in particular who would spend time alone and not join in the foolish behavior of the others. At dinner one night, I had gone through the serving line and was looking for a table. I spotted her across the room sitting at a table large enough to seat eight, and yet she was all alone. I went over and asked if I could join her. She glanced up just to see who it was and then looked down at her food again. "You don't have to sit with me," she said. "I know, I just need to talk with a mature person for a little while. These kids are a little noisy for me." I learned a lot about her. She was a senior in high school, worked part-time and was an honor student. She was extremely well spoken and had matured far beyond her seventeen years. She knew exactly what she wanted to do with her life and was secure in who she was. When I finished eating, she smiled and said, "OK, you can go now." She was perceptive enough to figure out my motive of giving special attention to someone who wasn't "one of the kids."

145

As for me, I was never really "one of the kids" either. The difference between this young lady and me was that I always struggled to hide it. I wanted so badly to be accepted, and many times I did things that I should not have done in an effort to fit in.

Once while flying high above the city in that airplane, it occurred to me that somewhere down there was a kid who would be like me when he or she grew up. I wished that I could locate and get to know him. I would tell him that listening is a good thing and that someday all that information might turn into wisdom. I would tell him not to be so concerned that he was quiet and withdrawn, and that when the time is right, he would bloom. I would tell him that God doesn't expect him to be perfect, just faithful to continue trying. I would explain as best I know how, that God uses circumstances and time to teach us great lessons if we will only be willing to learn. He would need to understand that waiting for God to do His perfect work in His perfect time would not be easy to learn. However, he would eventually discover that this kind of patience would be very necessary in order to experience the abundant life that our Lord offers. I would also tell him to hurry up...and learn to wait.

13

Hurry Up and Wait

The War of Patience

"You want what? You want it when?" Most of us are demanding when it comes to the things we want. We also find few who exercise patience in this fast-paced world we live in. At eighteen years old, I received my "crash course" on developing patience and it was a lesson truly learned the hard way. Over twenty years later, I found myself remembering it and coming to understand something important about God. During the time when I was dealing with the hurt, anxiety, and abandonment caused by my divorce, I wanted God to intervene quickly to restore my relationship with my daughter so that I would be able to move on. But that didn't happen when I thought it should. Thus, I was forced to recall this earlier time when things didn't go the way I wanted, nor in my time frame.

It was December 1965 and I was on a plane landing in Amarillo, Texas. As a new recruit in the Air Force, I was about to begin this lesson of all lessons on building patience. I had heard all of the horror stories about military basic training and so it was only natural that I had become very anxious. But my anxiety was reduced greatly by the nice sergeant who met three others and me, in the terminal. He was very polite as he helped us with our bags and made small talk as he drove us to the base. He pulled right up to the front door of our barracks and again helped as we unloaded our things. Sitting on the steps laughing and talking with several other guys my age was another sergeant. His green fatigue uniform was starched so that it looked as if it would break should you try to bend it. He had very dark complexion. He introduced himself as Sergeant Tenario. I decided by his name that he must be a Native American. I arrived at that assumption because it rhymed with Geronimo and of course because he certainly had the characteristics of a Native American.

He glanced at his clipboard and found my name. "Oh yea, Hudson. You are in 12 - B. Go on in and put up your things and I will tell you where to go to get something to eat." What a nice man, I thought. Just as I had suspected, the guys back home had told me a lot of stories about how mean everyone would be just to scare me. It had worked, but now I felt that this new experience would be fine after all. When I came back out, another sergeant was talking with Sergeant Tenario and said that he would walk over to the mess hall with us to have dinner. Now here was another really nice person. As we ate, we asked him lots of questions about what to expect tomorrow. He said that usually on our first day, we would have it real easy, just signing in, orientation, and getting our uniforms and such. That was another relief since it would give me another day to adjust to this new lifestyle. I couldn't help noticing that he ate very quickly and sat impatiently as I nibbled at my food. I told him that I was sorry if I was holding him up but I was a slow eater. He just smiled and said no problem.

That night as I settled in my room with three other guys, I thought this wouldn't be so bad. It would probably be like a camping trip. We couldn't go to sleep for quite a while as we talked about where we were from, our families, and our futures. Finally, I fell asleep thinking about how far I was from my home. I had joined up only about six months out of high school. Now here I was finally at basic training at an Air Force Base in Texas. Because of the Vietnam Conflict, basic training had been reduced to four short weeks. Thousands were being trained and shipped all over the world but mostly to Vietnam. As I lay there that first night, I really wanted to go home, but as I dozed off, I thought how bad can it be?

I've Landed in Hades

"Get up you worthless bunch of scum. What are you doing still asleep at this hour?" Startled, I rolled over in the dark and tried to see my watch. About that time one of the other guys turned on the light and said, "It's 3:30! Who's doing all that yelling?" It didn't take long to find out. Sergeant Tenerio walked into our room with fire in his eyes and he was grabbing everything in sight slinging it against the walls. As he left our room and moved on to the next, he screamed to the top of his lungs. "You've got fifteen minutes to get showered, shaved, dressed, your bed made and out front in formation." As I ran to the bathroom, I thought that this order would be impossible to carry out and was wondering what would happen if I didn't make it. Fifteen minutes later, I was standing out front in the dark with about forty-four frightened and bewildered young men.

Tenario came out to the porch yelling and screaming at us, and then he walked back inside again leaving us there for another fifteen minutes. Finally, he returned and I was wishing he hadn't. "I have never seen such a worthless bunch of losers in all my life," Tenario yelled out as he walked back and forth in front of our not-so-evenly-spaced formation. He moved from person to person screaming insults in our faces and telling us that he would either make something out of us or would ship us back home on a bus. "I'm going to be your mother, your daddy and your worst nightmare all rolled up into one. Now, we are going to march over to the mess hall and eat the Air Force way." He had some guys hand out flashlights to everyone so automobiles wouldn't run us down and we began our pitiful march. How could someone yell so loud at so many for so long and so early in the morning without losing his voice?

Whoops! We're Early

Finally, we arrived at the mess hall where we would stand until they were ready for us inside. We waited, and waited and finally someone came out and said, "It won't be long, they have started cooking now." By this time it was almost 5:00 AM and beginning to get lighter. I remember thinking, why didn't we just get up at 5:00AM or so and come down here by 5:30? That would have been just about right. In about another twenty minutes, we began moving through the door, one line at a time. We got inside and the food was thrown onto our tray with no consideration of what we wanted. Finally, I sat down and began to eat. I was never a fast eater and always ate each food on my plate one at a time. I was probably chewing my fifth bite when I heard that dreaded voice. It was Tenario. "Get up you lazy, slow, rednecks and hillbillies. You are not going to spend the whole day here eating. You will be outside and in formation in three minutes."

Three minutes later and still hungry, I was standing outside waiting for our sergeant. Fifteen minutes later, we were still standing there, but no sergeant. Finally, he appeared out of nowhere and began criticizing the way we were lined up. Then, yelling at us as if we had just shot his dog, he marched us half way across the base to get our hair done. You guessed it! They weren't quite ready for us there either, so we waited for at least forty-five minutes before marching single file into a fifteen-chair barbershop. I sat down and my barber asked how I would like my hair cut. I said to cut it kind of short so I will fit in. He kind of smirked as the clippers felt as though they were digging into my scalp. As I was leaving, I glanced in the mirror and almost fainted as I saw this totally bald version of myself.

There were several other stops that day, two more at the mess hall, and each one had something in common. We were hurried to each place only to find that we had to wait before we could go in. I soon learned all about the "hurry up and wait" method of driving new recruits crazy, which the military had carefully devised. It was very effective since several of our guys appeared to go nuts after only a few days. However, for those of us who stuck it out, it instilled in us a lesson of patience.

Liz and Zach

This "hurry up and wait" program is not unique to the military and it certainly isn't new. There are many examples that come to mind in scripture. Let's examine just one: the story of Zacharias and Elisabeth, father and mother of John the Baptist. Afterwards, I want to show you how all of this is relevant to one dealing with divorce and custody issues.

Zacharias was a priest and both he and Elisabeth were descendants of the priestly lineage. Both were described as righteous before God, walking in all the commandments and ordinances of the Lord blamelessly. But they had no children—Elisabeth was barren — and both were now considered old and past the age of having children. In that era, being a woman who couldn't have children was shameful and a man could put his wife away for that cause. Nevertheless, Zacharias remained married to Elisabeth and they were both faithful to God. Sometimes when people don't get what they want out of life and when they want it, they may give up on God and take things into their own hands. These two made a choice to be faithful to each other and to God because they trusted him. It is very hard for one who does not trust God to wait on him in faith.

Zacharias had been waiting patiently on God, remaining faithful, and always praying consistently. Most likely, it was always in his mind that he was getting old, time was slipping away, and he had no child. But instead of giving up, it appears that he prayed even harder. We read in Luke 1:13 that the angel of the Lord appeared to him and said, *"Fear not, for your prayer is heard; and your wife Elisabeth shall bear you a son and you will call his name John."* God was finally answering his prayer. But what was that prayer? Well of course, he was praying for a son. But there may have been more to his prayer than just that. We don't know for sure, but it is probably safe to assume that this priest was also praying for the coming of the Messiah. For many generations, Israel had longed and faithfully prayed for his coming.

Zacharias could have taken things into his own hands, divorced Elisabeth, and found him a young new wife who would give him children. If he had, he might never have had the privilege of being the father of this special child God would give him. This child would become John the Baptist, one with a very special mission from God. The angel described the son he would have in this way: *"He shall be great in the sight of the Lord, and shall drink neither wine nor strong drink; and he shall be filled with the Holy Ghost even from his mother's womb. And many of the children of Israel shall he bring back to their God."*

Zacharias had been good and faithful, but then one little weakness showed itself. He doubted what Gabriel was telling him and because of that, he lost his ability to speak until his son was born. Like the rest of us, he wasn't perfect. Faith brings a positive outcome, but doubt causes negative consequences. The writer of Hebrews says, *"Without faith, it is impossible to please God."* Faith demonstrates a trust in God's integrity. Zacharias had faith, despite his brief time of doubt, and he learned patience, which made him willing to wait on the Lord.

This child born to this old couple was well worth their wait. He was to become the prophet who would go before Christ preparing the way. He would convert hundreds, possibly thousands and also baptizing many including Jesus himself. Eventually he was martyred, beheaded, for the cause of Christ. Of John, Jesus said, *"I tell you the truth. Among those born of women, there has not risen anyone greater than John the Baptist."* To have a son like this was well worth the wait, worth being faithful for a long, long time.

It's How You Play the Game

There is another perspective that is worth looking at in this story. I believe that all good persons want to live in such a way that when they die, they will leave something behind worth remembering. In the scheme of things, our lives are hardly a blip on the radar screen of time. If we aren't careful, that blip will be so insignificant that it can't even be detected. Think, if you will of people you have known during your lifetime who are no longer alive. Some perhaps lived very long lives into their seventies or eighties. They have long since passed on and now we struggle to find the mark that they left on the era in which they lived. Were their lives wasted? Perhaps or maybe there was a series of small, seemingly insignificant things that they did while they were alive which made some impact on society and maybe even an eternal contribution.

In a world filled with so many diverse interests and causes, it seems that a great many people could make significant contributions in at least some way. Others could do much more, depending on their particular talents and on the extent to which they were willing to make an effort to benefit others. No doubt, many of them made their contributions in quiet ways that were hardly noticed and not long remembered. These contributions are just as real.

How do you suppose John viewed the achievements and the faithfulness of his father? It seems quite likely that he was aware that his father and mother had waited patiently on God for a long time. I believe that John had the privilege of seeing his father with two sets of eyes. The first was through a pair of spiritual eyes. The scripture we read earlier told us that John would be *filled with the Holy Ghost from birth.* I believe that would enable him to see how his father was used by God to bring into the world the one who would prepare the way for the Messiah.

Yet he was also able to see his father through the eyes of a son. When a child looks at his father, he should see someone whom he can trust and on whom he can depend in times of difficulty. He should see a protector, one who will stand between his child and any danger which might present itself. The child, when he has grown up, will become aware that his father is human with flaws and weaknesses like everyone else. But he will also recognize and appreciate those good things the father has been so careful to do. I can't help but believe that John saw his dad as one who impacted history in a positive way. He surely knew how long his parents had waited to have a son. He saw a dad who was faithful and willing to wait on the Lord for his best.

God wants all of us to wait for his best for us; it's we who want to hurry up and run out ahead of God. Several good lessons came out of my military experience that have been helpful throughout my life. I learned about self-discipline, submission to authority, and maintaining a good attitude even when things are not what I would like. But maybe the most valuable lesson was about waiting. I was forced to learn to wait... and wait...and wait. I had no idea at the time that this training would help me to learn to wait on God. Throughout my life there have been times when I acted impulsively, but when I did, the results were far less than God's best for me. There were other times when I waited and he revealed his way and his will for my life at just the right time. He has perfect timing; he's never early... but also never late. Isaiah 40:31 says, *"But they that wait upon the Lord shall renew their strength; they shall mount up with wings as eagles; they shall run, and not be weary; and they shall walk, and not faint."*

Not Yet ... Not Yet

God loves his children, and doesn't want us to have anything less than his best. He has prepared a plan for each of us and in his time will reveal the direction our lives should take. Until we understand what God's plan is, our role is to simply wait. Possibly the most difficult time to practice waiting on God is immediately after a divorce.

Often, a newly divorced person will quickly seek out a romantic relationship as a reflex reaction. It is almost as if we need to quickly validate our self-worth, and we think that finding someone who wants to be with us will do that. This is very dangerous and potentially destructive, not only to us but to those around us as well. Our children are especially at risk in these situations. They may become attached to this new person who has entered their lives only to have him or her disappear when the relationship runs its course.

It takes time for the emotional upheaval of a divorce to subside and for one to begin to think rationally again. The amount of time that takes may be different for each person. Just the same, seldom if ever would anyone be ready to enter into a new relationship soon after a divorce. If you had just finished running a marathon, would you immediately begin a cross-country bike ride? Of course not. Your body and mind need time to recover from the incredible stress caused by the very long run. Divorce under the best of circumstances is very stressful, and you need time to recover.

In the Bible, God says, *"Be still and know I am God."* (Psalms 46:10) Our problem is *"being still."* We often refuse to do this. *"Being still"* is waiting on God. So, consider this advice from someone who has tried it both ways; hurry up... and wait on God. The rewards are well worth whatever the length of time that wait may be.

When we are not willing to wait on God, we almost always receive less than his best for us. As we move into the next chapter, you will see just that. Some people have suffered severe consequences as a result of their impatience and bad judgment. You will also be allowed into their most intimate thoughts concerning their battles with divorce related issues. Now, lets go have some *Conversations with the Wounded*.

155

14

Conversations with the Wounded

Voices of the Embattled

In practically every war since the beginning of time, it has been customary for kings, presidents, heads of state, and generals to visit those who were wounded in battle. The purpose was to offer encouragement, show concern, and express deep gratitude for the sacrifice they had made for the cause. In addition, it was an opportunity for a leader to get first hand reports and vital information from the battlefield. From this information, an insight could be gained that could come from no better source. The wounded have not just been to the battle, they have been intimately involved and wear the wounds to prove it.

Ask most who have experienced divorce and especially those who struggled for custody of their children, and you will soon sense that they too were wounded in battle. Many have scars that have outwardly healed, yet are still sensitive to the touch. You have but to mention their former spouse, or in some cases their children, and all of a sudden their countenance changes and they may become withdrawn or sad.

As I have worked with and talked to the divorced over the years, it has never ceased to amaze me how close to the surface these wounds really are. Through directing and facilitating a divorce recovery program, I have seen persons come in who were freshly wounded and looking for a divorce emergency room of sorts. With them, it is just a matter of trying to survive the day. Their joy has been stolen. Their life may be in shambles, and they need to

157

know that there is hope.

Also, I have seen those who have been divorced for many years, yet have finally come to terms with the fact that their wounds had never been allowed to properly heal. Maybe they made the mistake of thinking that another relationship would solve their problems and heal them. By the time they get to us, many have been married and divorced several times. Each failure is but another wound added to those that had come before. Some have learned very late that through a real relationship with Jesus Christ they can experience true happiness, joy, and fulfillment. Others are still searching for answers.

I had an opportunity to talk with some people wounded in the battle of divorce. With their permission, I've written down their comments and answers to various questions about their particular struggle. As you read these interviews, see if you identify with any of these who have survived the breakup of their family and witnessed the death of their own dream. If you are just now contemplating divorce, note the pain and in some, the outright regret which they are still carrying.

ELEANOR

Eleanor is a talkative, bubbly, and attractive lady in her fifties who had been married to the same man for well over 25 years. In her words, her career had been performing the duties of a wife and mother and she really knew little else. It was a complete shock when her husband told her that he wanted a divorce. She felt sure that after having been married so many years, the dissolution of their marriage was not something either of them would ever consider. Once reality set in, emotions ruled her every day and she withdrew from life to the point of practically becoming a recluse. This went on for months until finally, at the urging of a friend, she showed up one Thursday night at our divorce recovery workshop. From the moment she began to speak, I knew that this one could be helped.

She was blatantly honest and spoke freely about her hurt and anger.

"I just want to kill both of them", she said. You see, she had discovered that the *"I just don't love you anymore"* excuse was just a substitute for the truth which is usually, "I found someone else who really excites me and you are getting in the way." A seasoned divorce attorney once told me that every time, without fail, a client sat across from him and told him the spouse had said, "I just don't love you anymore", that somewhere lurking in the shadows, was a third person in the equation. If the client chose to hire a detective, it would only take a few days to discover the identity of the paramour.

Eleanor was as angry as anyone I have seen and it took a few weeks of venting in our group, for her to begin to let it go. Finally, one night we were dealing with the issue of forgiveness and she had a breakthrough. That week she forgave her ex-husband and his new wife and sought reconciliation. No, not to re-establish her marriage, but rather to make peace and restore harmony with these two whom she had previously hated. Today, Eleanor is still wounded and struggles daily with the effects, which only naturally come with the break-up of a home. She lives alone with her teenage son and is working now to help him with his anger as he seeks to salvage his own life.

B E T H

Occasionally, someone will cross your path and leave you a much better person. I am just that because of a wonderful lady we will call Beth. When she first walked into our group meeting, she brought a lot of things with her. Yes, she carried some baggage from her failed marriage, but she also brought peace and joy with her. Seldom do we see someone who has done everything they could possibly do to keep their marriage together only to have it fail anyway, and yet are still together themselves. She was definitely together and an incredible encouragement to the other participants. Was she hurting? Had she been wounded? Had her whole life been turned upside down? Of course, but she knew Christ intimately and it was from Him that she drew her strength. She shed many tears in our sessions, but they were usually tears of compassion for someone else who was hurting. She had learned the secret of dealing with trials and disappointments long before she came to us. She knew that Christ was her one and only true source for strength and peace. But she had also learned that with her focus on her daughter and the needs of others, her own needs seemed to pale. She found great joy in ministering to others and it wasn't possible to do that if she was involved in her own self pity.

However, she did share with us some of the pain that she had experienced. First, of course was the rejection that comes from a spouse choosing someone new. But more hurtful to her than this was the heartache that her seven-year-old daughter suffered thinking she too had been rejected. Her daddy had left home and she saw that as him choosing to leave her, which by the way, is absolutely true. And then, there was weekend visitation. She said that from the beginning and even now, the child cries on Friday as she prepares to go to her dad's house for the weekend. She is particularly afraid of sleeping in a strange house with a dad in another room with a woman who isn't her mother.

It seems that Beth is doing everything right, but even so, she and her child are still suffering. Yet her hope lies in the One who set the stars in their place in the heavens. By comparison, it seems a small thing to ask that He set one's life back on course.

GRACE

Earlier in this book I talked about why a parent would choose to inflict so much hurt and anguish on a spouse and children. To place one's own selfish desires before the needs of the children is certainly something very hard to understand. Grace knows all about this having been one who has done just that and continues to pay for those decisions even today.

Married with two beautiful little girls, she was a person whom anyone would have thought to be a very happy young woman. But in her mind there was something missing and she thought that it could be found in her affairs with other men. She knew the risk involved, but to her that made it even more exciting. It was during one of these escapades, that she met a man who swept her off her feet making her feel very special and unique. It was because of her attraction to him that she chose to move out of her home and leave her family. When her husband found out about the affairs, he threatened her life. Frightened of what might happen, she decided to move 2,000 miles away with her lover. She got her divorce and they were married, but nine years later she discovered that he had been unfaithful to her. She had given up everything for a dream of what might be but that had turned out all wrong. Riddled with guilt, she had begun trying years before I met her to restore what had been lost. I asked her some pointed questions and these were her answers:

What was your reaction when reality set in concerning what you had done to your family?
"Guilt, and lots of it. How could I have been so selfish? I began trying to justify what I had done by telling myself that I had lost my own mother when I was young and I turned out all right. I also told myself that my children were fine since they were with the better parent, their father."

How is your relationship with your two daughters now?
"Both are teenagers with the older one being very understanding and close to me. My younger daughter has not wanted to talk about what I did to them. She seems to get very angry with me for seemingly insignificant things. I have wondered if

this is her way of lashing out for my abandoning her when she was so young. I continue to pray that she will be able to get past these suppressed feelings and that our relationship may be restored someday."

Where are you now in this process?
"I am taking it one day at a time. There finally came a time when I chose to give all of the guilt for deserting them to God. It was more than I could bear. There are times when I catch myself wondering 'what if ', but I also know that the damage has been done and my time will be better spent in working toward reconciliation with my girls."

How have you dealt with not being involved in the daily lives of your children?
"When I left them, my older one was six and the younger one was four. Not seeing them through these younger years on a daily basis was so very hard. I have missed many "firsts" in their lives. These are things that are forever lost and things I will never experience. Their father remarried and there was someone else now that they called "Mom". I can't express the depth of hurt that this has caused me. When I finally came to myself and opened my eyes and heart to Christ, He became my source for strength and it has been much better since. From that time till now, He has been my guiding light in both good and bad times."

How was visitation with your children?
"There were several months when I didn't see them at all since I had moved so far away. When I came back, I had regular visitation every other weekend as well as extended stays during summer months. I remember times when I drove for two hours to pick them up, and they refused to go with me. Then, I cried all the way back home ... alone. However, I vowed to never stop making the attempt."

If you could go back, what would you do differently?

"There was a time when my husband offered to take me back. I could have gone home to my kids, but I chose not to face what I had done. Instead, I chose to reject him and my girls one more time. That was a mistake I have had to live with for a very long time."

What would you say to someone contemplating divorce?
"Pray with your spouse. Pray with others whom you respect. God's plan is for children to grow up with both parents. Allow God to guide you, not the flesh."

Grace has come a long way and has learned from her life experiences. She is now involved in youth ministry and finds fulfillment and joy helping others. She still lives with regrets, but is coping and continues to face the challenge of each new day.

SHELLY

Life is full of surprises and one of those for me was a young teacher. In our group discussion sessions, she would normally sit very quietly as the extroverts shared everything of any significance and some that might be questionable. Occasionally, she would speak to an issue and it would usually be something profound. Throughout the weeks, I watched as she was transformed and became more out-spoken. Then, when I interviewed her for this book, I discovered how deep her thoughts really were. I hope that you will see what I mean.

At what level was their dad involved in the lives of your children after the divorce?
"Because of the type person he was, I expected him to fight for custody and at the very least be extremely involved in their lives. Once separated, he no longer had time for his children. The separation agreement provided that every second weekend and Wednesday evenings, he would have the children. He has

only picked them up twice on Wednesdays, and the weekend visits were often shortened to only one day. The children were heartbroken and missed him so much."

Did you encourage him to exercise his visitation?
"I tried several times, but these discussions always seemed to turn to angry tirades, and sometimes in front of the children. I saw them also becoming angry with both of us as well as each other. At one point, it became very difficult to get my four-year-old to go with his dad. Soon, there were less and less attempts on his part to see his children. Even phone calls from him were rare. This caused me to become angrier than ever with him, and I found myself "punishing" him by not keeping him informed about important events in the lives of his kids. Finally, he lashed out at me for leaving him out and I said, "If you had spent more time with them, you would know what was going on in their lives." I thought that since I had encouraged his visits with them as well as being very flexible with the schedule, the barrier between them had to be all his fault. But, how wrong this would prove to be! No matter how angry I was, I came to realize that as their mother, I had a responsibility to give them both of their parents. I vowed that there would be no more anger between the two of us and wrote him a letter calmly explaining how much they needed their dad. I also asked what I could do to help make spending time with the children easier. The next time he picked up the kids, there was a new calm and peace between us that felt very good to me and the children. It was then that I forgave him and decided to move on with my life."

How did this all turn out?
"He now sees the children on a regular basis and we have a civil, if not friendly, relationship. Our kids are healing and beginning to be the happy, loving little angels that they once were."

What would you say to someone contemplating

divorce?

"For me, divorce has been the most painful thing I have ever had to experience and it devastated me in so many ways. I was physically ill, an emotional wreck, financially distraught, and spiritually weakened. But as awful as it was for me, it was many times worse watching my children suffer. Seeing them hurt so much and not being able to relieve their pain, was a virtual nightmare. I had been in an unhappy marriage, but had no idea what misery really was. I would tell anyone thinking about divorcing, to do everything in their power to keep it together, and yes, for the sake of the children."

What advice would you give to someone who is hurting from a divorce?

"Find a support group as soon as possible. Expect a lot of pain, but know that Jesus Christ will heal you and make you whole again. I know, because He did it for me."

E L A I N E

Have you ever known someone who has "been there.... done that" when it comes to experiencing difficulties? Elaine has "been there.... done that" several times and has to be on guard against going there again. It seems that calamity has been a way of life for her and her family for decades. Now, in her fifties, she seems to be coming to terms with the way her life has gone. She is earnestly seeking God's direction to make sure the chaos is not revisited and peace becomes the norm rather than the exception.

Elaine, tell me about your children.

"I have three by my first husband and three by my second. All are grown now, except my youngest son who is in high school."

How is your relationship with your children?

"Very strained and distant on the better days. My youngest son and I are working together to restore what we once had. My ex-

husband has custody of him and they live in another state. When he comes for visits, I try very hard to be the mom he so badly needs and deserves. My other children have, for various reasons, written me off as their mom. I wish it were not so, but I can only hope that someday God will bring about healing and forgiveness so that we can become at least somewhat of a family again."

How have you coped with the alienation and rejection by your children?

"I have learned to cling to Christ and my church family. I cannot imagine what it must be like for someone to experience what I have without the support of Christ and fellow Christians. I have been in therapy over the years and although it has helped to be able to talk about and work through the many issues in my life, I have learned that Jesus is the "Great Healer."

What has been the deepest hurt that you have experienced through all of this?

"Without a doubt, loosing custody of my son. All of the other children were gone and seemed to want nothing to do with me. My son was all I had left to show for my entire life. When I received word of the courts decision to award custody to my ex-husband in another state, I thought I would die. I truly wanted to die and why not? I had nothing left to live for. Once I regained some of my composure, I decided to relocate to be near him. After living there for only three months, it became apparent that I should leave to allow my son the peace he needed. I moved back to my home state and I was alone again. Because of the expenses involved in the custody battle and moving, I found myself homeless. I lived with my sister for a while, stayed at the Salvation Army for three nights, then, I moved back in with my sister once more. It was during this time that she and I restored our relationship and I finally had at least one family member back."

What would you say has been the most significant positive change in your life?

"When I finally decided that I could do nothing right, I trusted God to take over the affairs of my life. I was led to a divorce recovery program where I made friends with whom I had so much in common. It was there that I learned to laugh again. I spent so many years involved in negative turmoil and hardly ever experienced any happiness. Now, because of the work that He has done in my life, I have true joy and actually laugh a lot."

What would you say to someone who is now contemplating divorce?

"Divorce is like an abortion ..... everyone involved is ripped apart and the effects are scarring and painful. At the same time, restoring a family once it has been through divorce, is much like trying to restore an aborted baby back into the mother's womb and give it life again. Only God can raise the dead and only He can restore a family the way it should be. Divorce causes irreparable damage to some, if not all, involved. Seek Christian counseling and exhaust every effort imaginable to keep your home together."

By the way, since my interview with Elaine, she has again moved to the city where her son lives and is working to restore their relationship once more.

Paul

I pulled up into the church parking lot an hour before time for our meeting to begin. I usually came early to set up and make sure everything was ready. I noticed a car with someone sitting in it. As I got out, so did he. "Is this the night for divorce recovery?" He asked. He was been waiting about thirty minutes before I arrived and there was still another hour before we would start. I had never seen anyone this anxious to begin a workshop. Over the next thirteen weeks, I learned a lot about Paul and he too learned a lot about himself.

Paul, do your remember the first night you showed up at our divorce recovery meeting?
Yes. I was actually very excited for a number of reasons. First, I was happy just to have some place to go. For weeks, I had gone to work, come home, and counted the hours till bedtime. My life was a drudgery, and I was just existing ... not really living.

For what other reasons were you excited?
I had spent hours thinking about my life, my divorce, and where I should go from here. I had seen the banner in the yard at the church and decided that a divorce recovery workshop would be the best place to start over ... to meet someone to start over with. I was certain that what I needed most was a new person in my life to replace the one I had lost.

What happened next?
That first night, there were some very nice ladies there and of course, I talked with them as the opportunity presented itself. However, as time went on, I became interested in what was being said and done. Slowly, over time, my interest turned from the ladies to the workshop and what was being accomplished there. I soon learned that I had originally come for the wrong reason. The last thing I needed was another relationship. I was a long way from being over my divorce.

It has been almost a year now since your divorce. What is your life like?
First, I look back at the state I was in during those first few months and wonder how I managed to survive. I was in critical emotional condition, and my every waking thought seemed to be directed toward my own problems. Now, I have moved on by beginning to regain my perspective. I have come to see that my relationship with Christ should be my first priority. Second to that is my kids. I spend every moment I can with them, and I know that if I had become involved with a woman, that would not be the case.

Where do you go from here?
That's easy. I go into tomorrow and do the best I know how while I am there. I continue to be a father to my kids and I serve faithfully the one who is responsible for getting me through this time in my life.

These are *"conversations with the wounded"* ... those who have been wounded by divorce. There are common threads that I am sure you noticed running through all of these interviews and case histories. First is the hurt. Some are hurt from what another has done to them and others by what they themselves did to someone else. This hurt in every case is deep, extremely painful, and has taken a very long time to diminish. Second, we see regrets for bad choices, which, in every case, affected the lives of themselves as well as others. Finally, there is agreement among all of those interviewed that Jesus has been the one in whom they found forgiveness, comfort, help, and peace.

Regardless of where one may be in the course of their life, we can all learn from these wonderful, but wounded people. They have shared their hearts to help someone else avoid the awful pain that they have experienced. For those who have had no choice in the divorce, these same people are saying to you that there is hope. There is life after divorce and it comes from a new or a renewed relationship with Christ. Give him your life today and watch as he helps you to begin again.

15

The Wonder of the Journey

Are We There Yet?

Taking a trip can be fun and educational. Tourists are sometimes interesting to watch as they seem to be fascinated by their unfamiliar surroundings. They will marvel at and take pictures of things that the locals fail to even notice. I suppose it's just the way we are when we travel as we take everything in, not wanting to miss a thing. If we are observant, there are many things to be learned on any trip we take. Our journey through life offers experiences that can be used to make our life better as we continue on our way. If we are traveling and have a flat tire, and then go to the trunk and find that the spare is also flat, we should learn that before we leave to always check our spare. Hopefully, from that time on we would never find ourselves in that position again since we have learned a lesson, right? Yet, there will always be new circumstances that challenge us; from each experience, we should be open to discover the right solution. This makes life so much more interesting. We should be enthusiastic about each new day and look for opportunities to learn as we take our journey through life.

I remember when I was a very young child, and my family was preparing for a vacation. When the time neared, everyone was busy packing and talking about what we would do when we arrived at our destination. We would be traveling slightly over a hundred miles, but to us that was a very long journey. My mom fried chicken and made sandwiches for the trip. Finally, we were off and as we drove toward Florida, it seemed that everyone was so happy. After a few hours my dad pulled over at a roadside park. I had never seen one before and I ran all around exploring every inch of it. Meanwhile, my mom was preparing our picnic lunch on one of the tables. Soon we were on the road again even more excited than before.

I was only about five years old then. I don't remember anything about the several days we spent in Panama City, Florida. What I do remember, and in some detail, is the journey there. I am sure that I ran on the beach, swam in the Gulf of Mexico, made sand castles and probably got sunburned. I just don't remember any of that. I only remember the journey. There must have been souvenir shops, floaties and rafts, the sound of the waves, and lots of other people. I can't recall those things, but I do remember the journey.

Life is an interesting journey. The journey is the wonder of life. It seems that we are always headed for one destination or another and when we get there, it was the journey that was most significant. As a child exploring that roadside park, I was amazed that someone cared enough for travelers to put picnic tables with small roofs over them for their use —and for free!

In my journey through life, I have been equally amazed at stops on the road. From time to time I have been in awe of people who cared enough for me to invest their time and even open their homes allowing me to be a participant in their families. I'm sure that it never occurred to them that they were making such an impact on my life.

Final Reflections

As I think of this, my grandparents come to mind. I can't imagine who I would be if it had not been for them. It was this wonderful couple whom I have patterned certain critical areas of my life after. It was with them that I felt safe. They were very predictable and though this may seem boring, to a small child predictability can be a good thing. I would never have wanted to make my journey without them.

There were also men of faith who have meant a lot to me on this journey. Pastor Burton Squires baptized me, discipled me, and helped me through the unexpected death of my father. Pastor Lloyd Mooney was my great teacher and stood by me during my custody ordeal. Tom Miller was truly a friend when I needed him during this same dark time in my life. He was an encourager and an inspiration not to mention a very fine pastor. It seems that every time I was really in need, someone would show up willing to help.

Earlier I spoke of having a flat tire and discovering that the spare is also flat. Let's say that this happens to you. You are all alone, it's late at night and you have no idea what to do. Suddenly someone stops and offers to help. This is the way God works in our lives. Every time I have had trouble on my journey, God has sent the right person at just the right time and with exactly what I needed at that moment. These people who were sent by God into my life were obedient to their call. Surely when God calls me, I could do no less.

One of the greatest blessings I have experienced on my journey has been the ministry that God has given me. Just as I can't imagine what this life would have been like without the help and influence of these wonderful people I have mentioned and so many others, not having the privilege of serving him would also be unthinkable. I have seen him take broken lives, rebuild them better than before, and use the experience of the brokenness to minister to others. Not only have I seen it, I have lived it myself. When I speak to a group of divorced men and women, I speak from experience. When I look into their eyes as they tell me about their rejection, loneliness, anger, unforgiveness, and feelings of hopelessness, I can truly have empathy because I was once where they are. As I see these emotions in their faces, I can tell them that with Jesus, there is always hope. I have had most, if not all, of the feelings that they are experiencing and have lived to write about it. If I can get through it, so can they.

Why Is This So Hard?

How does one ever prepare for a spouse saying " I just don't love you anymore and I want a divorce?" It's when this happens that we learn how much *"reality bites"*. It can cause one to practically go into shock and think "This just can't be happening to me."

Then, shortly thereafter when you wake up one morning to find yourself *"sleeping with the enemy"*, how can you make such a transition? Just a few weeks ago, you were waking up with the love of your life. Not only are you losing the mate you have loved so much, but if custody of your children does not go to you, you will be suffering another great loss. When you realize that as a non-custodial parent, you will be missing out on most of the daily wonders and joys of watching your child grow up, how do you manage to go on? All of a sudden you are literally out of the loop and can't seem to get back in no matter how hard you try. Through all of this you realize that the responsibility of being your child's role model hasn't gone away. It's still very important and must be maintained, but how can that be done when you are so seldom together?

Divorce is one of the most difficult things a person could ever experience. If it isn't, then something very serious is wrong and you need to examine yourself to find out why. If it doesn't break your heart, then the marriage didn't mean to you what it should have. When two people become husband and wife, according to scripture, they become one flesh. Divorce doesn't separate and restore them as they were before they married. It can't because they have been kneaded together like bread by their marriage. Instead, divorce rips them apart like the tearing of flesh, and part of one person is still attached to the other and vice versa. Emotions sometimes rule, and frequently, irrational behavior surfaces. Initial reactions include shock, grief, and placing blame. Not far behind is anger.

If not dealt with properly, anger can do irreparable damage. Being angry is a way of expressing our frustration of not being in control and capable of bringing order to this chaos. We pass through several stages during this time and each one is likely to bring with it feelings of anger. If we suddenly discover that we are lonely, that loneliness too may bring on anger. Our anger will usually be directed at the spouse who isn't there with us. It is because we are alone that we become angry with the person who is absent.

When anxiety presents itself because of the uncertainty of our future, that anxiety or fear, may also cause us to be angry. In such a time as this, anger is not inappropriate. This anger is called righteous indignation and simply means that a person is "justifiably angry". Jesus displayed righteous indignation when he cleansed the temple. It is a natural response that may be keyed by several other emotions. What is most important here is that we know when and how to express this type of anger. We should never inflict physical harm upon another person in the name of righteous indignation. Ephesians 4:26 says, *"Be angry and sin not."* Know how to control your levels of anger, and how to express it without sinning, even when it is justified.

Not My Job

If ever there were someone who had a "right" to be angry, it would have been the Old Testament character, Joseph. Because he was the favorite son of his father Jacob, his brothers were extremely jealous. They threw him into a cistern and then sold him into slavery. They covered up their sin by telling their father that a ferocious animal had devoured him. He was taken to Egypt where he served as a slave to Potiphar, the captain of the Pharaoh's guard. Here, he was falsely accused by Potiphar's wife of attempted rape and thrown into prison for several years. He was eventually released because of his ability to properly interpret Pharaoh's dream and given the position of second in command under Pharaoh over all of Egypt.

When the famine Joseph had predicted came upon the land, his brothers were forced to travel to Egypt to buy grain. As they came before Joseph, he knew who they were but they didn't recognize him. Here was an occasion for Joseph to be angry—righteously indignant. However, he chose to forgive his brothers and ultimately made one of the most profound statements in all of scripture concerning anger and forgiveness. In Genesis 50:19, he tells them, *"Don't be afraid.. Am I in the place of God?"* Joseph knew that God doesn't need our help in administering judgment for sin. Think of the relief one can have when the burden of "getting even" is not something that is an option since *"Vengeance is mine, saith the Lord."* Joseph had learned the blessings of forgiving and not allowing anger to control him.

Divorce can bring out the worst in us but we can also choose to allow it to bring out the best as well. Divorce under the very best of circumstances is extremely hurtful. The wounds are severe and healing can take years. For the divorced, waiting for God's healing can be incredibly difficult and unfortunately, many people don't wait. Instead, they find another person to become attached to. Not waiting on God can have devastating consequences. As we look at various statistics concerning divorce and remarriage, some show that over seventy percent of second marriages end in divorce. I feel that the main reason for this is that many people represented by this statistic did not allow enough time for God to do his perfect work of healing. It is a reflex response to attempt as quickly as possible to replace someone whom we have lost.

Through all of these trials, it is easy for our joy to be

stolen. There may be days when we wonder if there will ever be any joy and happiness in our lives again. I am here to tell you that *"Weeping endures for a night, but joy DOES come in the morning."* It will require some work on your part, but the joy will come again.

Once you have made it across to the other side, and stand looking back at your journey, you will see how God was working in every situation. The light will come on, the vale will be lifted and you will see clearly again. You will be stronger having been through the worst time in your life. You may think, "After this, everything else will be easy." As you stand and look back at your journey, you will see many people who have impacted your life. Hopefully, you will see many you have positively influenced as well.

Life is filled with opportunities to do good, even great things. With every tragedy, every disappointment, every heartache, comes an opportunity, not only to grow, but also to do a good thing—the right thing for others. How you respond to all of the facets of your divorce can demonstrate your firm belief that God is the answer. Don't allow your hurt and your pain to rob you of an opportunity to show forth the love of God to someone who needs desperately to see it.

Many Forks in the Road

Joseph had decisions to make on his journey through life. When presented with a choice to punish his brothers or to forgive them, it seems that to him, the question didn't even arise. His love for God and for his family was so strong that not doing the generous and forgiving thing was never an option that he even considered. I wish I could say that I had always made such good decisions on my journey. Quite the contrary. Many times I chose the wrong path in dealing with the emotions that raged within me. When this happened, the result was always negative and definitely counterproductive. When we react this way, there is much wasted energy which causes harm when it could be used to do good. Often there are words spoken that we cannot take back and things done that we wish we could erase forever.

While all of this is going on, there is usually an audience observing our every action and reaction. Friends, relatives, acquaintances and even strangers are watching to see how we will respond to the turmoil in our life. More importantly, our children are like sponges soaking up every word we speak, every act of anger at our spouse, and every seemingly insignificant negative gesture.

What an opportunity to teach our children wonderful lessons about how to deal with the trials in their own lives. If they should see us wronged yet not lash out at the person who wronged us, they may choose to respond this way when it happens to them. If we have committed a terrible act which has caused someone grief and we acknowledge it, ask for forgiveness, and turn from our wrongdoing, that will speak volumes to them about accepting responsibility for their own actions. The world is a huge classroom. We are either learning or teaching by every move we make through our lives. We are learning by observing others and teaching by what others see us do.

Careful Who You Ask For Directions

Advice is always in abundance when we are going through the hard times of our lives. It seems that everyone is an expert, an authority on practically every subject. You may get legal advice from those who may have never been in a courtroom. Some may tell you that you have to *"play dirty"*, since *"all is fair in love and divorce"*. And then there are those who seem to think that all you need is another relationship and that you need it now. They start parading the candidates by for your review before the divorce is even final...much less the healing is complete. All of these well meaning people obviously have no clue whatsoever about what is going on inside you at this time. Many just want you *"fixed"* at all cost so their lives won't be disturbed in any way. Learn to recognize that although some good advice may come your way, there also may be some which, should you act upon it; will be counterproductive and possibly even destructive.

It is at this point in the process that you need to be in a credible divorce recovery program. I cannot stress the importance of this enough since it can literally save you from making many very bad mistakes in your decision making process. Here you will find others who are struggling just as you are just to get through the day. Usually meeting once a week, most participants cannot wait to get there and receive the help and comfort offered at these sessions. There are so many wonderful aspects of good divorce recovery programs, but perhaps the greatest of all is that you will soon discover that you are not alone in your feelings. Others are experiencing the very same emotions and challenges that you are and each shares with the others how they are coping.

I can only recommend a sound Biblically based, Christ-centered divorce recovery program, which is usually sponsored by a local church. Through these programs, participants are introduced to Christ, the great healer and are shown how he can take a shattered life, put it back together, and use that life in a way that the person could never have imagined. Divorce recovery facilitators lead each group to understand that although divorce grieves the very heart of God; he forgives our failures in our marriage in the same way that he does the many others, which occur in our lives. If you are struggling with divorce and are not involved in a divorce recovery program of some sort, by all means find a workshop at a church near you and enroll immediately. That alone will greatly accelerate your healing and possibly avert another broken heart.

If I could go back to the point where my marriage started coming apart, I would do many things differently. Nothing is more important to me than setting a good example for my daughter. Yet in the midst of having one's life reordered, literally turned upside down, it seems that our emotions nearly always get the better of us and run roughshod over everything reasonable. We must guard against these raging emotions which cause us to lose control and drive us to do the very things we never thought we would. As we move through this life God has given us, we will impact everyone we meet in some way. We may leave them with scars or we may leave them with blessings. It's up to us, and usually it depends on how we handle our emotions.

This Too Shall Pass

Life truly is a fascinating journey. It is crucial that we learn to respond to its challenges in a Christ-like way. As we do so, we need to maintain a proper perspective. When we are suffering or having a very hard time, each moment seems as though it will never end, and it is so hard to see how brief our lives are as compared to eternity. We are told that from God's viewpoint, a thousand years is but as a day. Abraham understood this as he journeyed through his life. God told him to leave his homeland and Abraham began his journey *looking for a city which hath foundations, whose builder and maker is God."* From the time that God called him, he lived in tents being keenly aware that he was just a visitor to this world; that the days of his sojourning were brief, and that his home was in heaven—in eternity.

When we develop this kind of awareness of the brevity of our lives, we become able to react as Abraham did. We will understand that the trials we experience afflict us for only a short season, and that sooner or later they will pass. When they do, we can stand on the other side looking back at our journey and give thanks that we have made it through. We can also celebrate the growth we have experienced through our trials and be prepared to share it with others in need.

Each person has a different story to tell, and someone

out there needs to hear your story. If you are in the midst of your journey through a crisis, learn the lesson of a young man on his first vacation. Hard as it may seem, learn to relish the trip as well as the destination. Ask yourself at every turn how you can take what is negative and make something positive out of it. Ask what God is teaching you through your experience. You may be surprised to find that not only can you survive, but you might even learn to enjoy *"the wonder of the journey"*.

Who Am I?

Throughout the message that I have been sharing with you, we have taken a number of trips back in time. The purpose of doing this was to reach back and pull out of the past an event or memory that impacted my life. In sharing it with you, I have hoped to paint a portrait of a very ordinary person, maybe someone just like you. I have always wanted to excel in some way, even as a child. But, it seemed as though it just wasn't to be. I was an average student, an average athlete, and probably a less than average husband and father. But finally, something happened that changed things. I met Jesus and through Him, I became a prince, a child of the King ... royalty. Soon I discovered that I had also become a priest with many of the same responsibilities as the priests of the Old Testament. I was no longer "just average". I was finally someone special, not better than anyone else, but special just the same.

I came to understand that this was the first step in my most important journey of all; the one that takes me to my destiny. Since it began, and it began at my conversion, Christ has been re-making me into someone he can use to accomplish his purposes. I can't wait to experience whatever is next in my incredible journey. With each new day, it seems as though a very small piece of the puzzle is revealed to me. That puzzle, when complete, will show a life which began as only average, but came to be used supernaturally to accomplish good, and maybe even a few great things for the Kingdom. One of the things that causes us to realize what a great God we have is that even though we are so unworthy, he is willing to use us anyway. Had I not knelt and received Him as my Savior over twenty years ago, my life would have been a shameful waste.

Who Are You?

What about you? You may be reading this because your world has been shattered by divorce. If so, you have been seriously wounded and need to be healed. Before healing can take place as it should, please make certain that you really know this Savior of whom I speak. And even if you do, I encourage you to examine your relationship with him. Are you seeking after him with all your heart? If not, please do so even now. He wants to be your father and your best friend. It hurts him when his children ignore him and fail to spend time with him. I cannot imagine attempting to make my journey without having Christ by my side all of the way. Even when I thought I was all alone, I later discovered that he had been there all the time performing one silent miracle after another in my life.

Why not stop right now and pray asking him for his help and that he might reveal himself to you in a new and powerful way. Ask him to take control of your life and bring order to disorder, hope to a seemingly hopeless situation, and joy to a life of despair and sadness. Ask, and receive.

Congratulations! If you prayed that prayer and meant it, your life is about change and I believe that you will notice a new and fresh sense of hope. You have just begun a new journey, and you will never be the same. Never will you feel completely abandoned again, for Christ has promised that he will never leave nor forsake his own. There is one other thing that will be important in your new walk with Christ. The church is the body of all believers in Christ. It is made up of all denominations that accept

Jesus as the Son of God and our one and only Savior. The church meets in buildings, homes, sometimes tents, even outdoors. The church is not those buildings we see with steeples and stained glass. Instead, the church is the people who have chosen to repent and accept Christ as their Savior.

As one of the church, you should be drawn to be with others who believe as you do. Just as we have a desire to be with our family, we should also exhibit a desire to be with our church family. If you are not currently attending and involved in a church body, I encourage you to immediately locate a place where you can go and worship the Lord that you just made a commitment to. This would also be a place that meets on a regular weekly basis. Search for a church where the pastor and leaders believe that the Bible is truly God's word and has been preserved down through the centuries by God for instruction to his church, of which you are a member. It's here that you will begin to grow and mature, being challenged by what you learn and being held accountable by your brothers and sisters in the faith.

The Best is Yet to Come

My journey is only one of millions. We each have our own unique story that develops as we travel through this life. God would have us all learn great lessons as we go our way and use those to help others as they too struggle. There are miracles taking place all around us but many times we only see our current problem. May the scales fall from your eyes and may you begin to see clearly the wonder of your own journey.

Now for a nice surprise. When I told my daughter I was writing a book about our family, I was afraid she would ask me to write in the abstract, using fictitious names and circumstances, or not write about her at all. I should have known better. She never ceases to pleasantly surprise me. Not only did she agree to the format that I used, but she has taken it a step further. I think by now you have come to see that I love her more than my own soul and want to share her with everyone I meet. She asked to write a few words that express a different perspective on divorce, parental relationships, and faith. What you are about to read is from the eyes and memory of a wonderful child of divorce. It is with great pleasure and enormous pride that I introduce to you my beautiful angel, literally my heart—my precious daughter Casey.

16

A Child of Divorce Speaks Out

By Casey Hudson Angle

As I think of my Dad, so many things come to my mind. Perhaps, my fondest memories are from a time that seems now almost like a fairy tale. I was a very small child eagerly awaiting his arrival home from work. The door would open and I would run as fast as I could and jump into his big strong arms. He would swing me around and I would suddenly find myself sitting at what seemed like thirty feet in the air on his shoulders. As he went into the kitchen where Mom was preparing dinner, I sat there on my throne smiling and playing with his hair looking down at her. He would entertain me nonstop until dinner was ready and afterward, we seemed to always wind up on the living room floor, side by side with my head on his arm, sucking my thumb and watching TV. There was never a doubt that I was truly the apple of his eye and yes, I am still.

Growing up in what I thought was the perfect home with the perfect mom and dad, I was never aware of any problems in my parents marriage. They had done a masterful job of protecting me from whatever troubles they might have had. Sundays and Wednesdays were church days and I looked forward to them. Each year, we would take a nice vacation somewhere, usually Florida or maybe into the mountains and everyone seemed so happy. Both parents were always looking out for my welfare and I felt so very secure in this wonderful family.

My Mom was extremely protective and concerned

about my health and well being. It was she who was always checking my temperature should I say that I didn't feel well, taking me to the doctor, and making sure that I was playing safe. Dad, on the other hand, was concerned about my spiritual health and was usually busy helping me develop good character. I remember at five or six years old, going into my room with him and talking about Jesus. He patiently explained what it meant to be a Christian and to be saved from my sins. Then, he asked if I understood and I said "yes." We both kneeled beside my bed and it was that night that I prayed with my Dad and asked Jesus into my heart. From that day forward, the Lord has been with me, in me, and taking care of me. It was with his help that I was able to come through the worst days of my childhood.

I was ten years old and it came out of nowhere and when I least expected it. I could tell that Dad was very upset as he sat me down and tried to explain that my Mom wanted a divorce. I couldn't believe it. How could anyone ever want to give up what we three had together? I was devastated and ran into my Mom's bathroom where she was doing her hair as she prepared to go somewhere. I screamed "Why?" as I cried uncontrollably. "Why do you want a divorce?" I just couldn't understand any of this. Why would she do this to us? I don't remember her answer, probably since it wouldn't have mattered anyway. I felt that my life had been destroyed. She left shortly after that for the evening.

Finally, after I had calmed down, Dad asked me if I wanted to come live with him. He said that my Grandmother could stay with us, but in order to make that happen, I would have to move with him to the town where she lived. This would mean that I would be changing schools. What was I to do? How could I live with my Mother since she was the one who was doing this to me. Without hesitation, I said, "Yes, I want to go with you Dad.'

Just a few days later, he awoke me very early in the morning and we took some things leaving my Mom still asleep. I looked at my room as I left and somehow knew that nothing would ever be the same again. We were only moving about an hour away, but it seemed like worlds apart from the home that I had always known.

My Dad quickly purchased a very nice house with a large back yard complete with a swimming pool. I was enrolled in school there and began making new friends. As I came home from school one day, I was to get a wonderful surprise. He had asked my aunt and cousins to redecorate my room complete with a beautiful canopy bed, which I had always wanted. They had turned a normal bedroom into a beautiful fairy tale for my Dad's little princess. He had made every effort to make this new setting my home and a child's dreamland. How could any little girl in her right mind ever want to leave this paradise?

A few weeks later, Mom wanted to have me for the weekend. I returned to what had been the only home that I had ever known, and all of the wonderful memories of my early childhood began to flood my mind. I must say that it felt very good to be back in my old room filled with all of my things. I had also missed her so much and the friends that I had played with for years as well. And then it began—the "tug of war". She was saying how much she missed me and how wonderful it would be if I lived with her. She explained how a little girl needed her mother. Finally, it was time to go back to my Dad's and I didn't want to leave. Perhaps it was partly because I felt so bad for her since she was all alone now. I reasoned that at least my Dad had his family, but she had no one. It was then that I decided to change my mind and to live with her.

The permanent custody hearing was scheduled several weeks away. It was during this time that the very worst memory of my childhood took place. I loved my Dad so and knew how much that he loved me. How could I possibly tell him that I didn't want to live with him anymore? He had done so much and tried so hard to make me happy, how could I tell him? Well, I couldn't. I did, however, tell a friend who told my cousin, who told my Dad. I have never seen him so hurt in my whole life. He took me for a long ride and asked me if it was true. It was here that he truly showed me how much he cared. That was the first time I had ever seen him cry. He couldn't understand why and kept asking me, but I couldn't give him a reason. I didn't know myself. I felt so terrible about the way I had hurt him. Honestly, I still feel bad about it. He had tried so hard, and it was as if I didn't care.

Soon afterward, I was in the judge's chambers answering his questions and telling him that I had changed my mind, wanting to go back with my Mom. I was ten years old and making decisions that no child should ever have to make.

Soon, my Dad was picking me up every second weekend for visitation and he did everything imaginable to make it fun for me. Looking back, I can see how selfish I was. From the time I would get in the car, he was asking me what I wanted to do, and of course, we would do it, whatever it was. Many times my choice would be to spend the night with one of my friends or at least have a friend spend the night with me. If I could go back, I would appreciate that I had a dad that wanted to be with me as much as possible. I suppose that kids can really be self-centered.

After some time passed, going with him every second weekend became a drudgery. I hated packing and leaving my things, my phone and my home. Also, my Mom was much more lenient, allowing me to do most anything I wanted so long as she knew where I was. Dad, on the other hand, wanted to spend time with me. When I got old enough to go out, he gave me what I thought was a very early curfew on Friday night. He wanted me to stay home on Saturday night so I would feel like getting up and going to church on Sunday morning. Sunday school and church was never an option with him unless I was sick. It just seemed that there were a lot more rules with him than with my Mom. I developed a very bad attitude toward him and being with him. The truth is, it wasn't he who had changed, but rather me.

The bad attitude began to fade as I grew into a more mature teenager. The older a child gets, the more she begins to think about what is really important. I began to realize that there had been many times when Dad would drop everything, no matter how important, just to be with me. He always wanted to be with me. There was never a time when he said, "I can't pick you up this weekend. I am going out of town", or "I have something else I need to do." He planned his life around my availability. I became aware of the difference in my Dad and those of many of my friends. Then, slowly things began to change again. I now wanted to spend time with him, and we would create things to do together. We went on trips and vacations out of town. I would call him to pick me up and take me out to dinner and as we sat there eating, talking and laughing, we renewed what we had when I was a little girl. I could no longer get on his shoulders, but I could hold his hand and I could kiss his cheek.

Now, many years later, we are not only father and daughter, but we are also great friends. Not a day goes by that I don't think about him. He is my confidant and I tell him everything. I go to him when I need guidance and advice on any subject. I know of no one better on earth to pattern my life by than my Dad. He has truly proven himself over and over by being that perfect role model. It has been by watching his life that I have come to know what it means to be a person of character.

Well, I am married now, and both my husband and I come from broken homes. It is because of this, that we realize how difficult it is to have a strong marriage. Many times, we will talk about it, and each time we vow to stay together and work very hard to strengthen our marriage. We don't have any children yet, but hopefully we will someday. When that happens, because of the wonderful example set by my Dad, I know that I will be a much better parent. I will make sure that my children know what a wonderful person their grandfather is. I can only hope and pray that they look upon their parents as I look upon my dad—as their heroes.

Conclusion

One hundred years from now, people may look back at this era in an attempt to define it. Some may call it the epoch of the electronic revolution. Others might argue that it was the age of spiritual hunger and quest for enlightenment. Some will say it was a time when information became more important than ever before.

As I thought about this, it occurred to me that we might be remembered as the generation that abandoned marriage and the traditional family. What a tragedy that would be! Yet it seems as though we are well on our way to that very end. There are many abominations taking place in our society today, each one bringing great harm upon all of those touched by them. However, of all the awful things that are happening, I believe that divorce may ultimately be the one that is causing the most damage to our families, our nation, and our world.

Earlier I said that if divorce doesn't break the hearts of both spouses, then the marriage didn't mean what it should have. If the marriage didn't mean what it should have, then it was because there was a lack of commitment. If we are to diminish the tragedy of divorce in our society, then we must determine to put real meaning back into our wedding vows, understanding the seriousness of the moment and the ceremony.

Our state lawmakers should be called upon to make pre-marital counseling a requirement for obtaining a marriage license. They should also be pressured to reform current divorce laws making it more difficult to get a divorce. The Covenant Marriage Law has been passed in Louisiana and is a very good beginning. Many are working now in other states to get them to follow suit as this new way of reinforcing the marriage commitment spreads across the country.

The responsibility, however, must not be solely that of our lawmakers. The Church should also accept its role in the movement to strengthen marriage. Our pastors and other ministers must begin to refuse to perform the ceremony until the couple has received an acceptable level of pre-marital counseling. Also, they should consider thoroughly the consequences when asked to unite professing Christians with non-believers. Premarital counseling is a wonderful time to discuss the issue of faith with a non-believer and offer that person an opportunity to accept Christ as Savior.

Our clergy must be firm and clear in the premarital counseling sessions and in the ceremony about the grave and solemn vows being taken. These steps, together with an effort to incorporate the couple into the supportive activities of the Church, could go a long way in preventing the tragedies that occur when marriage is taken lightly. It is most important that the church should be actively involved in helping couples to get their marriages off onto a solid footing. The Church must also offer support and guidance in the search for solutions for those whose marriage may be in trouble. So many of our political and religious leaders seem to have their heads in holes like ostriches while our families are dying. In Psalms 69:20, David writes:

"Reproach hath broken my heart, and I am full of heaviness; and I looked for some to take pity, but there was none; and for comforters, but I found none."

What an indictment this is against our leaders and against all of us who could step forward and offer help. The brokenhearted walk into our churches every Sunday looking for some to take pity, and for comforters. I am convinced that many times, they find none. In many churches, the divorced are shunned, ignored, looked down on, and treated as someone having a plague. If it is a plague, it is now one that is thriving even within the Church itself. How greatly we need to come to terms with it, learn to fight against it, and to comfort those who have been wounded by it.

We now have a generation of young adults who cannot remember when divorce was rare. Fortunately, I can and I have vowed to work wherever and however possible to help others regain the vision of intact families as the norm rather than the exception. Let me challenge you to join with me and the many others who are beginning to work in this crucial cause? With God's help, we can turn it around. With his help ... we can resurrect the dream of one man, one woman for life. With his help ... we can prevent *"many a tear"* from falling.